Paid in Blood

**Lock Down Publications and Ca$h
Presents**
Paid in Blood
A Novel by *Hood Rich*

Paid in Blood

Lock Down Publications
P.O. Box 870494
Mesquite, Tx 75187

Visit our website @
www.lockdownpublications.com

Copyright 2019 Paid in Blood

First Edition June 2019
Printed in the United States of America

Lock Down Publications
Like our page on Facebook: Lock Down Publications @
www.facebook.com/lockdownpublications.ldp
Cover design and layout by: **Dynasty Cover Me**
Book interior design by: **Shawn Walker**
Edited by: **Tam Jernigan**

Stay Connected with Us!

Text **LOCKDOWN** to 22828 to stay up-to-date with new releases, sneak peaks, contests and more…
Or **CLICK HERE** to sign up.
Thank you.

Like our page on Facebook:

Lock Down Publications: Facebook

Join Lock Down Publications/The New Era Reading Group

Visit our website @
www.lockdownpublications.com

Follow us on Instagram:

Lock Down Publications: Instagram

Email Us: We want to hear from you!

Submission Guideline.

Submit the first three chapters of your completed manuscript to ldpsubmissions@gmail.com, subject line: Your book's title. The manuscript must be in a .doc file and sent as an attachment. Document should be in Times New Roman, double spaced and in size 12 font. Also, provide your synopsis and full contact information. If sending multiple submissions, they must each be in a separate email.

Have a story but no way to send it electronically? You can still submit to LDP/Ca$h Presents. Send in the first three chapters, written or typed, of your completed manuscript to:

LDP: Submissions Dept
Po Box 870494
Mesquite, Tx 75187

DO NOT send original manuscript. Must be a duplicate.

Provide your synopsis and a cover letter containing your full contact information.

Thanks for considering LDP and Ca$h Presents.

Hood Rich

PROLOGUE

I stayed low to the floor following the music, when I got to the living room, I couldn't believe my eyes. The room was decorated by candles, which really set the tone. Tim and Moe were sitting back on the couch while, and this is what I couldn't believe, Binkey danced in the middle of the floor so seductively that for a moment I got caught up in the show. She wound her body like a snake, clad in only a red thong and matching see through bra. She turned around with her back to them and made her ass clap before hitting the splits and bouncing up and down. Then, she was on all fours popping her pussy, causing the material to wedge itself between her lips. I was so hard and mesmerized I had to snap out of that shit before I lost my bearings on the situation.

I ran up to the couch and smashed the handle of my gun into the back of Tim's head and whipped the wire around Moe's neck in one quick motion. Tim fell off the couch and Binkey kicked him in the chin, knocking him out instantly. Moe tried to pull the wire from around his neck with no success.

"Punk, stop struggling before I kill yo ass, nigga put your hands down or I'ma choke yo ass to death." He complied.

After we tied them up, I interrogated them about li'l shorty D. "Say, do one of niggas know what happened to them shorties that got gunned down last week? I advise somebody to speak up or its gon' be two more dead bodies on this block. Now one of them kids was a little girl and she was like my lil sister. Somebody shot her eight times for no reason. Somebody better tell me something, speak up!" I looked back and forth between the two men. By this time Tim was woke and Binkey

7

was back dressed. They both remained silent. I looked at Binkey, "Do your thang, ma, these niggas think its a game."

She jumped up and stuffed a rag into Tim's mouth. Then she produced her machete', swiped and sliced his ear off and tossed it on to his lap. When he saw his ear, that nigga's eyes got so big, all I heard was him screaming. Binkey laughed and sliced his other ear off and his time threw it on Moe's lap. Before he could start hollering, I pressed the .40 Glock to his forehead.

"Nigga, you bet not start screaming. Now, who the fuck killed my lil sister? You niggaz run this block, somebody know something."

"Man, I don't know who bucked them shorties, joe. Me and the homie was trying to figure that shit out ourselves. I swear to God, I don't know. I -"

Binkey stuffed a rag into his mouth, then sliced off the tip of his nose, then a chunk off each one of his cheeks. I pulled the gag out of Tim's mouth, while Moe screamed into the rag.

"Listen, bro, we been beefing with them niggaz in Englewood. They came through here spraying two days before that, they must have come back and wet the block up again. They want this turf over here, saying we clocking too much money."

"Who is the niggaz? Give me some names!" I demanded

"Moeshe and J.J. calling shots for them niggas over there. They been sending li'l shorties over here to wet the block. Your lil sister must have gotten caught in the cross fire, that shit ain't got nothing to do with us."

Binkey stuffed the rag back into his mouth, walked behind him and cut his right hand off and tossed it on to his lap. "Bitch Nigga, that's for grabbing my ass."

He was screaming into the rag and I couldn't help

laughing. That was the reason I loved this girl so much. I swear one day I was gone marry her ass. Wasn't nobody else more perfect for me than she was. I turned to Moe and shook my head. I pressed the .40 to Tim's forehead, telling him to stop all that fucking screaming, then I took the gag out of Moe's mouth.

"How much money y'all got in this ma'fucka? We ain't looking to kill nobody, all we want is the dope and money, then you niggas can go. So, where the shit at and how much?"

Moe was silent weighing his options, he saw Binkey walking toward him with the rag and started to spill his guys. "We got two bricks in the pantry and a hundred and fifty thousand in the deep freezer. I got ten gees in my drawers, and that nigga got ten gees in his. I'll show y'all where everything at just please keep that crazy bitch away from me with that blade."

I ran all over the house following his directions, when everything was recovered and bagged in pillow cases I let Binkey do her thang. Watching this part always made me hard for her.

Binkey took her machete and stood in front of Moe first, she walked around him in circles and stopped right in front of him again. I was wondering what she was doing, and I got my answer quickly. She was staring him right in the eyes, respecting the rule of always look a man in the eyes before you kill him. In one quick motion she whipped her arm through the air and began slicing, first his face, then his chest and finally she was behind him trailing the blade from one ear to the next. After she killed him, she stuck her hand inside his open mouth and cut his tongue out, tossing it on his lap.

"That's for snitching and giving up your stashes so easily." There was a look of disgust on their face. I knew she hated snitches. She had lost her brother when eight

9

members out of his crew snitched on him. They gave him life in the feds under the R.I.C.O. Act.

Before she could get to Tim, I pressed the barrel of my .40 to his forehead and squeezed the trigger twice, splattering the back wall with his brain fragments. Binkey looked at me as if she was completely pissed off. I didn't care, we had already spent too much time on this job. I grabbed the pillow cases and we jetted.

Chapter 1
Seven

I couldn't help purging my guts over and over again. I had been on my knees for the last hour unable to stop gagging, sweat poured from my forehead and tears rolled down my face. I had never felt weaker or been more broken. I felt like the room was constantly spinning around me. My thoughts were jumbled, and I could not wrap my head around my reality.

My beautiful and precious mother had just passed away after battling the deadly cervical cancer. She had been fighting the illness for three years. One minute, the doctors swore that she had beaten it, then the next they were re-diagnosing her all over again. Finally, after going through so many trails and tribulations with three different doctors, my father stepped in and hired my mother a personal physician that tended to her every need around the clock.

Three months later, she was supposed to have been in full remission, and absolutely cancer-free. Two months after that news, my family was shattered and making her funeral arrangements. Nobody fully understood what had taken place so quickly. One minute she had been so healthy and strong, the next she was gone.

I rocked back and forth on my knees with my head pointed toward the ceiling, tears running down my cheeks. I could not suppress the groans from escaping my throat. I had never been hurt so badly before in my life. My mother was my everything. She was the motivation behind so many of my life decisions.

It was because of my mother that I had chosen to stay in school and pursue my dream of playing professional basketball. Every time I saw my mother sitting in those bleachers or in those stands wearing my jersey it made me go so much harder. When I made a shot, I could hear her cheering the loudest, when my team lost, she always rushed to give me the biggest hug, and the softest peck on the cheek. She kept me so strong and focused. I didn't know what I was going to do without her, I did not know where I would find my strength.

There was a loud banging on the bathroom door. The noise shook me out of my zone and caused me to wipe my mouth with the back of my hand. As another wave of nausea settling over me, I took a deep breath and tried to center myself.

"Baby, please open this door and let me wrap my arms around you what else am I here for?" Kendra whimpered.

She sounded like she was on the verge of tears herself. She and my mother had been real close. Kendra made it her business to call my mother every night before she turned in. They often traveled to my basketball games together, and when I got a full scholarship to play college basketball at the University of Wisconsin, they had both took turns giving me kisses all over my cheeks as if it was some sort of competition.

Kendra and I had been dating for three years and there was no doubt in my mind that one day she would be my wife. I fell in love with her every single day, and her loyalties never ceased to amaze me. She started beating on the door again, snapping me out of my zone.

"Seven, baby please, I got Brittany on the phone and she breaking down just as hard as you and I don't know what to tell her." Her voice began to break up. "Baby, please, I'm freaking out."

I took a deep breath and blew it out. My knees were wobbly as I attempted to stand. "Kendra, baby, I'm okay, I'm just trying to get myself together, give me a minute.

But, listen, I need for you to stay on the phone with my sister until she calms down some. Tell her that I'm okay and that I want her to come down and see me as soon as possible. Do you hear me?" Tears were already leaving my eyes again. I could hear her sobbing through the door.

"Yes", she whimpered weakly. "Baby, can you please just open the door so that I can be in your arms?"

In the three years that we had been together, I had never allowed her to see me express any weak emotion. I had always been the strong one for the both of us. She had always leaned on me for strength. I did not know how she would view me after she saw my tear ridden cheeks.

I tried my best to gather myself. I ran a wet face cloth over my face and smacked my cheeks lightly trying to bring life back into them. Once I figured I was as put together as I could possibly be. I opened the door and she fell into my arms, wrapping her own arms around my waist and burying her face into my chest. I tried to be strong, but I wound up breaking down all over again.

We fell to the floor with our arms around each other. My sister Brittany was sniveling on the phone that laid on its back between us. I knew that she was all alone, probably in her dorm room sitting in the dark. I switched the phone over to speaker.

"Brittany, little sister, are you okay?"

I heard her hiccup, before answering. "Hell-low, Seven, is that you?" Her voice was barely above a whisper.

"Yeah sis, listen, I need for you to be strong. We all have to be, we have to remember how our mother raised us to stand tall and never fold."

"Seven, I know, but I miss her so much. I need her right now, it's not fair, she should not be gone. Our father brought in the best doctors, he promised us she would be okay, but now she's gone!" Brittany wailed.

I hugged Kendra tighter, as she heard Brittany's breakdown she started to unravel. Her tears were soaking through my shirt, her groans were getting louder and I felt her nails digging into my waist.

"Brittany as soon as classes let out tomorrow, I want you to drive here and spend the weekend with me. Do you hear me?"

She was quiet for a few seconds. "Yes. I'll be there."

"Sis, please be strong and know that I love you, okay?"

"Okay. I love you too." She whispered.

That night, Kendra and I held each other while we reminisced about my mother. Although I thought it wouldn't, chatting about my mom actually helped me feel a little bit better. After three hours we were finally able to drift to sleep while playing one of my mother's favorite singers, Keith Sweat.

Although the coaches told me that I could skip practice the following day, I declined. I felt I had to be there, besides; balling was one of the things that helped me clear my mind. So, I showed up and showed out. Every play got an extra effort from me. I practiced like my mother was sitting there in the stands watching me like she often did when I was in high school. Afterwards, I would get hugs and high fives from the entire team, and everyone gave me their condolences, even the coaches. It made me feel a little better. Knowing that the team had my back was great, I felt as if I had a second family.

When I came out of the locker room Kendra was waiting for me in the hallway. As soon as she saw me, she ran up to me and wrapped her arms around my neck,

"Hey, baby, you looked so good out there." She said

then planted a juicy kiss on my lips.

She smelled of black orchid, her Dred locks fell neatly behind her back. It always turned me on how she stepped on tippy toes to capture my lips with her own. She made me feel strong.

"Yea, thanks boo, for some reason I was just feeling it. Every shot fell and each play coach called I felt like I could see it forming, so I met my marks head on."

"The whole school is talking about you entering the Draft this year. Are you even considering the NBA next year?"

I smiled. "Who knows, we gotta get through this wild ride in the NCAA tournament first, then I'll make my decision. She took a step back and slapped her hand on her hip. "Don't you mean we'll make a decision, you know, as in – you and I?"

I couldn't help laughing. "No doubt ma', you're right, you and I together will decide if we're ready to enter the NBA Draft." She smiled, walked back to me and on tippy toes, leaned in and sucked all over my lips.

I carried both of our bags to her truck and tossed them on the floor in the back, then settled into her passenger's seat and snapped my seat belt around me. That's one thing that the University police did not play about. If they caught you rolling without your seat belt on, you were getting a ticket, there was nothing you could do about it. Kendra slid into the driver's seat and started the engine on her Land Rover. I always thought she looked so good with her small frame, pushing a big SUV. No sooner than the engine turned over did she have "Jhene Aiko" bellowing from the speakers. That was her favorite singer, and she was starting to grow on me too.

She pulled away from the curb after adjusting her mirrors. "So baby, are you at least starting to feel better?"

I shrugged my shoulders. "I'll never get over losing my mother, but I knew I gotta be strong because that's what she would want."

Kendra nodded. "That's right. She was a strong woman, so we have to honor her memory and not weep in sorrow."

It was just like Kendra to always be the voice of reason. No matter what situation we found ourselves in, she could always find a way to put a positive spin on things. I loved being around her when things were tough, because she always helped me to see another angle.

I looked her over closely and noted that her small skirt had climbed up her sexy caramel thighs. She looked over just in time and caught me staring, that didn't stop me from reaching at and rubbing on the exposed flesh. She smacked my hand. "Baby, stop, and why is it that every time you come back from practice you are always so riled up?" She smiled sexily. "Aren't you supposed to be abstaining in preparation for the big tournament?" she teased.

"Yeah, I am, but boo, I think I gotta break that rule. I need some of that essence girl." I was rubbing her thigh again. It felt so soft and tender under my hand.

"Come on now Seven, we've been over this already."

"Kendra, we been together for more than three years, when are you gone let me bless this body?"

In the three years that we had been together, Kendra and I had not gone all the way. We had done everything along that road, but we had never quite succeeded in arriving at that special destination. She was serious about her principles.

"Seven, you will bless this body on our wedding day. I love you, that is a fact, but I love myself more. I value my temple and I feel like a man should not be able to enter it until he is ready to be with me in holy matrimony. I cherish who I am, and I would think you'd appreciate that within your Queen."

I nodded. "Damn boo, that's deep, you're right I just love hearing how you break that down. Nevertheless, we still gone do some road traveling tonight. Right?"

She smiled, then licked her lips. "Right."

***

I was awakened at two in the morning, Kendra had just left no more than fifteen minutes prior to the beating on my front door. I looked through the peep hole and saw my sister Brittany. I opened the door and she fell into my arms. As I wrapped my arms around her while we sat on the couch in my living room, she laid her head on my chest and told me what was on her mind.

"Seven, I hate being all the way down there at the University of Milwaukee, I wish that I could be closer to you, especially now that mom's gone. She was the only one that visited twice a week."

I kissed her on the forehead, "Don't worry, I'll start coming down there. I miss you just as much as you miss me. Have you spoken with Roman or Heaven lately?"

"No, you know they are too absorbed in the streets of Chicago to pay attention to anything else. I always found it weird how even though we are all siblings, we have chosen to separate in pairs."

"Yeah, I know. Well, no matter what, me and Kendra will be down there to see you twice a week from now on."

She picked her head up and sucked her teeth. "Kendra, why her? Why can't you come alone? You know I don't like her."

I pushed her head back down to my check. "So,

What's new? You don't like no female I mess with, don't let me find out that you're jealous of her." I teased.

She shot her head up again. "Jealous, please! She ain't got nothing for me to be jealous of. Don't think that just because she ain't giving you none that that makes her a better woman, because I'm telling you now, that chick is looney." She twirled her finger in a circle around her head to emphasize her point.

I laughed. "So, you gone stay with me tonight, or are you driving all the way back to Milwaukee?"

"Do you promise to hold me the whole time?"

I nodded. "I got you, sis."

She smiled," I still don't like Kendra."

Chapter 2
Roman

When I got that phone call, I was sitting in my den alone playing chess against myself. If a nigga ain't hip to doing that they should start, ain't nothing like learning how to capitalize on your own mistakes. Once you become familiar with those personal mental battles, you can transfer those skills on to the streets where real life mistakes a rust yo ass. You see, every chess piece to me resembles an obstacle or enemy. I try and conquer both sides. I never play for a stale mate. With every move I'm always trying to mate myself and most importantly, I never cheat myself, to me this shit is beyond serious, on that board is life or death, and I'd rather meet death than lose in life. Fuck that.

I never been the type of nigga to do churches, and even though I love my mom's more than life, the demon in me still wouldn't make that exception. I said the majority of my goodbyes alone in the morgue before they came and took her body away to be embalmed. I kissed my Queen seven times on her forehead and once on each cheek. I let her know that she meant the world to me and that I would never forget her, and she would never be replaced. I made sure she knew how much I appreciated her and every sacrifice that she had ever made in honor of me and my siblings. I told her that I would hold the family down. I couldn't promise the support would come from nothing legit because moms knew I lived by that sword. But I did let her know that the road would be paved with good intentions.

I left the morgue and the light breeze of spring slapped me in the face. It was well after midnight, yet the streets of Chicago where busier than ever. Friday night, and for the first time in years I wasn't thinking about popping bottles or fucking wit a bunch of hoes. I was thinking about getting this bad taste out of my mouth. This taste of missing my mom. I knew the only way I could even begin to feel somewhat better was to wet somethin'.

I called my pops and after going through the unpleasantries and reminiscing about my Queen we finally got around to business. "Look, Pop, I need to pop something off, my brain is racing a million miles a second and I ain't gon' be able to focus on shit until I feed the beast, so tell me what's good?"

He asked me where I was, and I told him to just meet me at the McDonald's a block away from my pad. When he pulled up in his big Excursion truck, he was dressed to the nines in an Armani suit, with the Mauri Gators. The suit all black with a baby blue bow tie, the trimming the same across his Gators.

Pops was always fitted, everything he wore was Armani, which is where he got his name from along time ago. Him and my mother had not been together in ten years, yet they were still married, and he always did everything that he could to hold her down. One thing I respected about my old man was the fact that he'd always drop whatever he was doing at the drop of a hat to be there for my mom, which was saying a lot because my Pops was a street nigga. Pops had his hand in everything from heroin to cocaine, from stripping to prostitution, and from loan sharking to murder for hire. The old man was a jack of all trades. As fucked up as that resume sounded, I was on the path to being just like him.

"As Salamu Alaikum, Son." He spoke as I climbed into his truck.

"Wa Alaikum Salam, Pop." I returned, still snacking on a few fries out my bag. I hadn't eaten anything in damn near two days. Sometimes my mind raced so much I forgot to take care of the simple things. I was still a lil cocky nigga though. I'm a hundred and eighty pounds, six foot even. My body stay ripped, cause whether I eat or not I try and greet every morning with calisthenics right after my morning Salah. That's something else I never missed was that morning Salah. Yea I'm a grimy nigga, but I still send my praises up to Allah.

"Tell me son, what's on your mind?" He leaned his seat back and sparked a gas filled Cuban cigar. Soon as the lighter hit the bud, I caught a contact and after one pull my old man started coughing. I laughed at that.

"Pop, I know you having trouble with them lil niggaz on 53rd and Carpenter. Tonight, I wanna go over there and change a few of they asses."

In Chicago, when the word change is used on some beef shit, that means murder. You gone hear the words changed and changed over a lot. That's Chi talk, that's where I'm from and that's how we get down, so don't lose ya self.

"Son, I already got somebody working on that. I don't wanna put you in harms way. What you need to do is to go home and rest your mind because you seem like you haven't had a decent night's sleep in weeks.

I immediately snapped. "Pop, look whether you give me the go ahead or not, once I finish this Quarter Pounder with cheese, I'm finna go over there and cause some ruckus all by myself. You can miss me with that 'you ain't trying to put me in harm's way', Pop, I'ma G, that shit don't bother me one bit, only reason I ain't just do it without your blessing was because of the respect I got for you, but truth be told, I don't like them niggas either. So, this is personal." My chest was rising and falling rapidly. I was geeked up.

"Calm down lil Moe. Look, I was gone pay fifteen

bands to have them aired out, but since you my son I 'ma pay you an even twenty to take care of your business tonight, just be careful and make sure you call me when you get back home. I can't really stand for something to happen to my first born." He leaned over and kissed me on the forehead.

That was just like Pops though, always trying to sap up the moment and plant his kisses all over a nigga. "Pop, fifteen's cool. This is business, you ain't gotta cut me no extra deals because I'm your son. Them streets out there ain't gon' cut me no slack, so you ain't suppose to either. How you sayin' that you don't want nothing to happen to me, but you trying to coddle me like I'm Heaven or Brittany?" I felt myself getting vexed, so I jumped out of his truck and took gang ways all the way back to my crib.

It was Friday night, so it was the norm for Y-Ketta and Pouchie to be throwing a party. These niggas were well into their thirties, but they still thought throwing house parties was the shit and for the most part with these kats it was because they ain't throw your average, everyday, run of the mill party. These studs went all out. It was guaranteed to be a fuck fest, with plenty strippers roaming through the pad from wall to wall. Ma'fuckas was gone be footing all kinds of powder and popping more different colored pills than Skittles. Molly was always on deck, and bitches was going, meaning they was giving up that body, if only for the night.

I pulled up on the block and there were already cars lined up. Plenty ma'fuckas had champagne bottles in their hands, Dutches behind their ears and a dimed-out stunna on their arms. The ladies that turnt out were something to see, and trust me, you could damn near see everything they had to offer because the shit they had on was a poor definition of clothes. Shorties had on daisy dukes so tight that it took practice to be able to walk. Biker shorts that promoted camel toes. The majority of them had on see through halters, or fish net tops that put their titties on display. This definitely wasn't a party where the shy was invited, and what's crazy is that this same party took place every single.

I looked around for a second, just parked, taking the scene in. It never occurred to me that I was about to fuck up these people's night. I just didn't give a fuck. The pain going on inside of me, over missing my mother, was eating at me like acid. Nothing mattered to me more than getting that feeling to dissolve because it was tearing me up inside.

As I said before, my Pops got his hands in a little bit of everything, now what brings Y-Ketta and Pouchie on his list of niggas to get rid of is the fact they were becoming prominent members in the extortion community. Home boy nem' had shit sewn up all over from Washington Park all the way down to Jackson Park. Every cent that they made was profit because they ain't have nobody they were paying dues to in Chicago which is unheard of. Everybody in Chicago gotta answer to somebody else. That's just how the game goes. Yet these two knuckle heads thought that they could change the game up and make their own rules. Six months ago, they were running under some dude named Twin, who was fucking with this white broad in Markum. It was through her brother that Twin was raking in a hundred jars a day and getting that shit off. Twin was paying dues to my Pops. He respected the game and knew that my old man had those blocks he ate his meals on, so he followed the guidelines according and paid homage. After he got knocked, his lil brother Pouchie took over the operation and hit the ground running. Pouchie was all about that paper, but he was also a freaky ass nigga.

The stud would pop them pills four at a time and be down for whatever, and by whatever, I mean exactly that. The streets said he'd pop that heater, but was a lil bit reluctant, and that would cost him.

Y-Ketta, was his right-hand man. Everything Pouchie did, he followed suit. A few broads back in the day was screaming them niggaz was more than friends. Kim said that she had been apart of their manage trios before and she felt left out. She said the nigga, Pouchie, got more dick that night than she did. Two nights later, her buddy confirmed that. A week after that revelation both hoes came up missing. I really don't give a fuck what these niggaz sexuality is, all I know is that after tonight that x-business would be turned over cause both of these niggaz time had run out.

I tucked my .40 Glock into my waist band of my Red Monkeys, flipped my all black tee over the handle, slid my hunter's blade into the small of my back and tightened my belt. Then, I hopped out my black Charger and blended in with the crowd that was heading into the duplex. It seemed like there were more women who turned out then men.

At the door I noticed one of the lil homies from the hood. I gave him dap and nodded. He pointed toward the party letting me know that it was cool for me to enter. I looked behind me and he and ten other lil homies were patting everybody else down. Damn, if they only knew that they had just let death into the party. I shrugged my shoulders, one thing a ma'fucka could never do was cheat death. When its time for your ass to go, then its just time to except that shit. For Pouchie and Y-Ketta, their time was up, and I was sent to make sure of that.

The party was cracking, blasting that Nicki Minaj 'Anaconda' out the speakers. The disco light made everything seem like it was moving in slow motion. I hated those lights, they always fucked with my stomach and made me feel nauseous. But I mastered that slight discomfort asap. I was on a mission so I pressed further into the party. When I got to the living room, I saw a bunch of niggas in a circle and in the middle of the circle were eight broads. They are competing shaking them asses, putting Nicki to shame. I've never seen a broad do some of the things that these hoes were doing. That shit had me rock hard, I had to snap out of it and get back to the task at hand. So, I slid on through the crowd and made my way upstairs. I went up the back way and as soon as I got up there, I saw the nigga Pouchie. He was standing up against the wall with a thick ass red bone in front of him giving him tongue while she stroked his penis that was completely out of his boxer hole. She dropped down to her knees and swallowed the whole thing while he stood up on his tip toes plunging into her mouth at full speed. I looked around and there were about thirty people upstairs and they were all engaged in some kind of sexual activity. *This shit gone be easier than I thought.* By the looks of his movements, I could tell that he wouldn't be long.

"Aaaarg!" And I imagined he began feeding her his seed. She got up off her knees and disappeared into the party. I definitely remembered her face, and I already had it in my mind that I was gon' get me some of that boss head real soon.

Pouchie staggered, caught his self against the wall, then made his way downstairs getting ready to walk past me as I stood right by the doorway. I grabbed him and wrapped my arm around his neck as I stood behind him. Then, with all my might I tightened the grip and fell to the floor with him with my legs around his waist, me on my back and I choked him while pulling upward. I saw my mother's beautiful face flashing through my mind.

25

Then, as his bones began to snap, I pulled harder and tightened my grip. I imagined her body in the morgue and all the pains of her death made me snap his neck. When his body stopped struggling, I released him. Without giving one fuck, I simply drug him to the bathroom, threw him in the tub and closed the shower curtain. Everybody was so doped up; they never even looked our way. Now I had to find Y-Ketta, that shouldn't be that hard since him and Pouchie were basically joined at the hip.

I found him when two broads came out of the upstairs bathroom naked. He was yelling something at them which couldn't be heard over Nicki Minaj spitting. After he said his piece, he turned to go back into the room and that's when I tapped him on the shoulder. He turned around, acknowledging me and nodded what up. I leaned closer and told him in his ear that I needed to holler at him. He nodded again and we walked into the room. Clearly, this nigga must have been tricking hard because he had twenty-dollar bills all over the room as if a piñata' had just exploded. On the floor I noticed that a small safe the size of a mini refrigerator at the head of the bed was ajar. When we closed the door, the loud music was finally drowned out.

"Whud up, lil homie?" Y-Ketta asked as he sat on the bed. He reached over and grabbed a mirror that had four lines of cocaine evenly spaced on it. With a rolled up twenty he tooted the lines up real hard then asked me if I dabbled.

"Naw, homie." With that I upped my Glock .40 and place the barrel right on his forehead. "Nigga, my Pops told you to pay dues, instead you chose to follow that stud Pouchie, now I gotta change yo ass."

Y-Ketta started whimpering and turned straight bitch. "Li'l homie, come on man don't kill me. You know

I just had a daughter; my baby needs me. I ain't never disrespected your old man. I was following Pouchie, come on man. Look, I got a hundred thousand in that safe right there, plus Pouchie got eighty gees in his, just take that and give it to your old man." He dropped down on his knees and crawled toward the safe throwing the stacks of money out of it while real tears trailed down his cheeks. By all means, I watched the nigga closely while he loaded all that bread into two pillow cases. Pouchie's safe was in the wall inside the closet. I made homie empty that one out too. Then, I had him lay across the bed on his stomach with his arms out at his side.

"Come on man, I gave you more than enough money to give to your Pops, can't you just let me live? I swear I will never come after you! We can make it like this night never happened, please man!"

The nigga's crying is what made me jump on his back, pull his head up by his dreds and slice his neck from one ear to the other. The whole time I was envisioning my mom's suffering. To me that nigga was cancer and I was killing it.

Hood Rich

Chapter 3
Heaven

"Bitch, you got the game twisted, before I ever put a dick in my mouth you best believe that that nigga gon' have dropped some nice bread. Pussy ain't free and neither is head. That's what's wrong with you hoes, y'all got the game fucked up and allowing theses niggaz to bust nuts for free!" I said.

"Yeah, girl, I guess you right, but a bitch can't always charge a nigga for the pussy, what about when you fienin' and you just gotta have that shit?" Kelly asked.

We were in my beauty shop and I was giving my girl some micro braids and I was almost done. Every time we were together, we always found ourselves having a crazy discussion involving trifling ass men. Kelly was a straight sucka for some good dick. You hit that bitch off proper and she was good to go. She had been my homie since the sixth grade. And ever since her first kiss, all it took was a little physical affection from a boy and she was head over heels in love.

I was finishing up the last braid. "Girl, still, you can never let a man know that you fienin' for his ass. If you do that you wind up giving him all the power you ever had. Once a nigga knows that he got yo ass strung out, he flips the script on you. That nigga gone go from lovey dovey to straight gangsta and start treating you like one of his conquests instead of the queen that you are. You see a man will always pursue that which is unobtainable, it's in his nature to do so, so until the end of time that's what he gon' do."

Kelly nodded her head as if she fully understood the science I was kicking to her, but I seriously doubted that. I mean don't get me wrong, my home girl was very intelligent, she was just a sucka for that pipe. She was like most women who allowed that joy stick to run their lives, so it really wasn't no sense in me trying to drop jewels on her because I knew that she would never take heed.

"Damn girl, you got my shit whipped." She marveled at her reflection in the mirror smiling from ear to ear. "This shit looks natural sis, damn you good at what you do."

I smiled washing my hands in the sink. "Girl you also gotta thank them Peruvian people. I put that Peruvian Remi in your head, that's one hundred percent human hair, that's why it's shining so much."

I looked her over and my homie did look good. It had only taken me about two hours to knock them braids out. I was perfecting my craft. One day I wanted to be more than a professional. I wanted to have my signature shops all over the Midwest and I know that now this was my only shop, but it be popping. Bitches be coming all the way from Indiana just to get their wigs done, and I had a team that met every challenge, so all of my customers left with that stamp of approval.

I grind so hard because I want to be a business woman just like my mother was. She scraped and saved to open up her first restaurant and raised four kids at the same time. She didn't let the world, or nobody's statistics tell her no. She fought her way forward and stayed determined and did everything that it took to make her dreams a reality. I honored her for that, and that's where I get my drive from. I refuse to lose.

After braiding Kelly up, I was sitting in my back office when Pam came and stood in the doorway looking me hard in the face. Pam is light caramel, about five foot seven, and a hundred and thirty pounds. The sista had long thick dreds that were parted down the middle and hung to each side of her pretty face.

"Why you looking at me like that?" I asked suspiciously.

She slapped her hand on her hip, still staring at me without saying a word. She took a deep breath and blew it out harshly.

"So, what, you just gone stand there without saying nothing? Oh well, you ain't hurting me, I can sit here all day. I ain't gotta be nowhere no time soon."

She came further into my office and closed the door. "Heaven quit playing, don't tell me that you forgot what today is?" She almost looked hurt. She began biting on her bottom lip nervously.

I played the fool. "Girl, what the hell you talkin' about cause you got me lost." I leaned back in my chair, pretending to be filing my nails, avoiding her eyes.

She lowered her head. "Damn sis, outta everybody I just knew that you'd be the one to remember." She turned to leave.

"Bitch you betta quit playing. Huh" I reached across the table and handed her the four Trey Songz tickets, along with the back stage passes, and the V.I.P key card that would get her into the hotel party that was taking place directly after the concert.

Her eyes lit up. "Aww Sis, you remembered. Oh my god you remembered!" she ran around my desk planting kisses all over my cheeks and neck. She hugged me so tight that I couldn't breath.

Now for those that don't know, I'm a lil chick, I'm only five foot three, a hundred and ten pounds. So right then sister girl was damn near smothering me. "Awright Ma, let me go girl damn. You already should have known that I would never forget about your birthday. You ain't just my employee, you are like my sister, don't come at me like you come at the rest of our Hen-house.

"She smiled and hugged me again. "You already know you coming with me to meet fine ass Trigger! Damn that nigga so fine!" She was ecstatic.

I pulled up in front of my son's school just as he was coming out the front door. I saw him hug some lil girl, then give her a kiss on the lips that lasted way too long. *Oh no he didn't*! I know I ain't just witness my baby give away no kiss to no lil stanky girl. He waved bye to her and she watched him all the way until he jumped in my Cherokee.

"Hey, Momma." He leaned over and kissed me on the cheek. "How was your day today?"

I scrunched up my face, a lil bit jealous. "My day was fine. Now tell me who that li'l girl was that you were kissing all on? Then you gon' come and transfer her germs on to my cheek. Who is she?" I asked watching the lil mixed girl hop into a Benz truck.

He laughed playing it off like it wasn't a big deal. "Mommy, that's my girlfriend, her name is Elizabeth and she's the head cheer leader at my school, and the prettiest." He added smiling.

My eyes bugged out of my head. "Excuse me, lil boy, but you are only twelve years, who did you get permission from to be calling some lil big head girl your girlfriend?"

He smiled, showing me both of his lil dimples. "Momma you just jealous, even though you don't got no reason to be, you know that I will never think nobody is prettier than my mother."

He continued to look out the window I noticed until his so-called girlfriend was driven away, only then did he look at me and shake his head.

"Boy, I know you did not just call me jealous, I ain't got no reason to be jealous ,whenever you think that she ready to do all your laundry and cook your meals you make sure you let me know."

I drove away from the curb and turned back up my India Arie. Whenever I was feeling stressed all I had to do was put her on the air waves and sister girl made sure she got me right. I loved everything that she sang about. It's like she was my distant sister from another mother. But we both had the same soul.

"Baby are you ready to go and see your father tomorrow?" I looked over and saw my son fidget in his seat. I could tell that he was wrestling with the question. He was trying to find a way to answer it that would be appeasing to me.

"Yea Ma' I'm ready. I just hate going through that whole process where they gotta feel all over you and feel all over me. It seems like they be doing everything in their power to make it so we never wanna come back again. Then they always talk to us like we don't even have a brain. I just hate the whole process.

Now you know it gotta be messed up for my twelve-year-old son to be spitting at me like that. It's truly amazing how children pick up on the craziest vibes in life. I was caught because we had never had this conversation before. My baby was no longer a little kid, he was in fact a young man and on the very verge of being a teenager. I could only imagine what was going on inside his brain. I knew that no matter what I told him that nothing would diffuse the fire raging inside of him other than the truth, and the truth was that I didn't even know exactly when his father was coming home. I just knew that he didn't have life. You see men never factor in all the things that we have to go through when those white folks take them away. They never see this side of the coin. It's in these moments that we single mothers can fully lose our child all together just by saying the wrong thing, and I wasn't about to jeopardize my relationship with my son for nobody. He is my baby and all that I have.

"You know what son? When we go and see your father tomorrow you can go and ask him exactly the same questions you just asked me, and we'll allow him to stand before you as a man and keep things real with you. Okay?"

He nodded. "Yes ma'am." Then smiled. "Thank you, Momma."

Chapter 4
Tariq

"Aww shit, Akki, I'm already knowing any time you get to doing plenty push ups that you finna hit that visiting room, so what's good, who coming to see you?" Peety asked.

I continued to do my diamond push-ups, trying to knock out a hot thousand before my baby momma got there with my son. I had about an hour and a half before they arrived, and I was already on seven hundred. I wasn't solely doing the push-ups to get that ripple effect; push-ups had a way of calming down my nerves and relieving my stress. Ain't no secret, every time I had to see my lil man under these conditions, that shit broke me down. I been in this ma'fucka ever since my seed was born. I ain't even have a chance to make it through the whole pregnancy with his mom's because they snatched me up a week after we found out that she was pregnant. Heaven was only seventeen then and I was nineteen.

I continued to push up and down feeling that stinging in my arms. "My old lady and my son coming I ain't seen my lil man's in about a month so I'm anxious." I grunted.

Peety got up and did a goofy ass dance, kicking his leg out like Michael Jackson, moon walking, spinning then out of no where his crazy ass hit the splits. "Ow!"

I fell flat on my stomach, rolling. This nigga was crazy. It was impossible not to laugh. You mix his goofy antics with the fact that homie is ugly as hell, you ain't got no choice other than to crack yo ribs laughing. He was dark skinned and looked just like Dave Chappelle. Just as skinny and everything. He had been my cell mate for two years now, and although he was a confessed drug addict, to me the homie was cool as hell and down for

35

me like a muthafucka. Every time some shit jumped off, Peety was right beside me with that blade, down for whatever.

His people broke bad on him before he even got to the county jail. So, my mans was going through the ringer, trying to survive in the belly of the beast. I took to the homie right away. Even though I ain't got much, my son's mother keeps me straight, her and a few other lil friends I got. Not to mention, I hustle hard in here. This joint is full of brothas that are trying to escape the reality of their current situations, so me being me, I find ways to capitalize on of that. They call me the pharmacist, cause no matter the prescription, I find a way to get that shit.

After my man got done dancing a jig, making me feel all good and shit, I grabbed my fresh prison greens, underwear and slipped into my shower shoes, headed to that water. "Look, Peety, while I'm up top visiting hold this package down for me." I handed him my work wrapped in lil bits of plastic.

With no hesitation, my man's grabbed it and tucked it in his draws. "No doubt li'l brother, I got you. You want me to buss a few moves for you while you up there? Or shop closed?"

"Man, dawg, you know how we get down. Be smart, and never pass up no money. Never hustle backwards." I gave him a pound, and he nodded.

As soon as I came through the door, I saw Heaven's bow-legged self walking toward the table where my son sat, just about to pop a piece of gum into his mouth. After twelve years she was still flawless. Caramel skinned, the face of an African Barbie, and jazzy as a rich heiress. My son looked around, then wound up looking toward the front where he knew I usually came from and saw me. He jumped up from the table and ran at me full speed until he crashed into me and wrapped his arms around me. My son said how much he had missed me and couldn't wait until I came home. Damn, every time he said those words it always caused my flesh to crawl. This was my only child. I hated being away from him. I hated watching him grow up through photographs and visits. I hugged him tighter and signaled to the guard letting him know that before the visit ended, I wanted to take pictures. He nodded in understanding.

"Damn boy you still fine as hell. Look at you looking all Army strong and stuff. Give me them lips." Heaven wrapped her arms around me as I pulled her in close feeling that body heat.

Our tongues danced circles around one another, then I sucked on her thick bottom lip, feeling my manhood starting to peak. After kissing for thirty seconds, we finally broke apart. I noted that both of her nipples were hard and showing through her Dior top.

"You still taste as good as ever." I rubbed her cheek then we went and took some pictures together. After we sat back down, I couldn't keep my eyes off of her nice thighs, and I saw a nice portion of them cause her dress was purposely pulled up to about mid-thigh. It wasn't exactly indecent, but we kept it border-line. Ma' always knew what I needed. She wasn't a rookie to this prison thing.

"Dad when are you coming home?" Tarig Jr. blurted out before I even had a chance to gather myself.

"And I don't want no supposed times, or no I might be's. I need to know when you are coming home exactly, I am old enough to know the truth, so please just be honest with me." He left his chair and stood right in front of me, his eyes pleading for the truth and nothing less than that. I took a deep breath and turned toward Heaven, who gave me a smile to show her sympathy.

Her look read that I had better give him the truth or I'd be in trouble. I turned back to my lil man and kept it real with him.

"Son, right now I got a total of eight years left to do. I'm eligible for a program that will help me get home in five. And right now, I got my sentence modification in hoping they will reduce my sentence to about three. But, as of right now, I have eight more years to do if all goes bad."

He stood in front of me trying to process the information. I saw him turning the numbers over in his head. His face was confused at first. Then, all of the sudden it was like he got it. "So that means that you won't be home until I'm almost twenty. But if you finish your program, I'll be seventeen. And if you get your time reduced, I'll only be fifteen?" He raised an eyebrow.

I could not believe how smart he was I nodded to let him know that his math was correct.

"Aw dad, that ain't that bad. All my friends were telling me that you had life and that you weren't ever coming home. As long as I know that you're coming home sooner that later I can deal with the pain of missing you. It was imagining you never being there that was getting the best of me." He reached and wrapped his arms around my neck and hugged me tight. "Dad I love you so much. I just want you to know that I'm going to be strong for you and my momma."

I was silently thanking Allah for my son's strength. Thankful that his moms was as one hunnit as she was. I had to get the fuck outta prison. I could clearly see that my son needed me. My throat got dry and I was at a loss for words.

"See baby, it wasn't that bad. Now at least our son knows exactly what we're up against. It's just for you to

Paid in Blood

take care of yourself in here so that you can make it home to us. You understand that, Tarig?" Heaven reached out and touched my hand. After the visit, my mind was fucked up. This was the first time I'd left them feeling like I had the weight of the world on my shoulders. I couldn't believe how my lil man took that information. Was he really growing up that fast? I remembered, like it was yesterday, the first time I held him in my arms. Now, I was having grown up conversations with him. It was crazy how time flew.

"What up, Ankh? Peety stepped to the side so I could step into our cell. I began taking off my visitors' greens, still kinda caught in my own parallel universe. "Tarig"

I shook my head, snapping out of my zone. "Yo, whud up, Peety?"

"How was the family lil brotha?" He was eating a bag of Doritos.

"They doing good, man. My woman still fine as ever. And my son getting taller and more intelligent. He asked me some grown man questions and recognizing and respecting that he had became I gave him some grown man answers. I respect my queen so much for how she is raising our Prince. I honor that woman man."

Peety nodded. "That's what's up." He reached under the bed and pulled out about dollars worth of canteen. I looked down at the bag and saw everything from cosmetics to Halal summer sausages. "While you were up-top, I popped about eighty worth. The Native head down the way say he gone send twelve hundred to that P.O. Box, too. Here go the rest of your work."

He handed me the goods and I gave him dap. "Good looking homie, you can split that canteen down the middle, you know I got you, my dude."

39

Hood Rich

Chapter 5
Scooby

As soon as I woke up my body was not feeling right. My throat was dry. My nose was running, and I had to piss like a mothafucka. I turned to my side and looked down at the woman who was sleep right next to me. Damn, she was ugly. I had to be fucked up last night to sleep with that beast.

After taking a long comforting piss, I washed my hands and found myself sitting at the table in the dinning room. I sat a fifty piece on the plate, broke it into fours and loaded my pipe taking a long hard blast and holding it in until I felt that my chest was gonna bust. After three more of them, I was lifted.

All my cares were taken away. I felt like me again. I don't give a fuck what nobody says, I love smoking crack. I love how it makes me feel and how it calms my body down, I don't think that there is any drug out there like it, and if it is I ain't chasing around to find out. The pipe is where my heart is. Just as I was loading up another piece, the beast woke up and came into the room with her hair everywhere.

"Good morning, baby, I see you trying to start the day without me." She came over and started to rub my back. I guess she figured it was a way to get into my good graces. Trick no good.

I pushed her away from me. "Girl gone and get away from me, you fucking up my vibe." I spat, starting to get irritated. Wasn't nothing like somebody trying to fuck with you when you were just trying to vibe alone.

"Aww, come on baby. I know you not gone smoke all that in my face. Didn't I break you off proper last night? Don't I deserve at least a lil taste for all my hard work?" She tried to sit on my lap and wrap her arm

41

around my neck.

I sat up and flipped her ass on to the floor. She landed with a big thud, looking up at me like I had lost my mind. "Bitch, get yo dirty ass off of me. Last night was last night, that shit ain't got nothing to do with right now." I looked her over, disgusted. Nasty bitch. I couldn't believe I slept with her ass. What the fuck was wrong with me?

"So, you just gone play me like that?" She was pissed. "Scooby, you forget that I'm the one that sat out there turning them tricks last night for you to even get them pebbles. Now you gon' act all stubborn and shit." She got up and rolled her eyes. Dusting off the dirty cut off shorts. Walking around with a dingy white bra. "alright, remember I got the pussy between my legs. I'm always gone be able to get right. You the mafucka that need me and not the other way around."

I dropped another piece into my pipe and blew that shit to the moon. I was on cloud fuck what this bitch was talking about. She may have had a point, but I knew that as long as I was alive and addicted to crack, that by any means I was gone find a way to stay high. Whether this bitch was apart of my life or not.

She turned around on her heels. "Baby please, can I just have a little hit? Just give me something to wake me up, so I can get my day started. Pleezee." She begged.

"Damn Sharon! Here!" I tossed her about a twenty piece and she damn near did a back flip in the air to catch it. When she did, she had the biggest smile on her face. She had the nerve to kiss me on the cheek and tell me she loved me.

I had to break camp. I jumped in my beat-up Buick Century and rolled out to my main blood's crib. I knew that he would be up and at 'em, and ready to go make some money. As soon as I pulled up, his girl was just coming down the porch. She wrapped her arms around me and gave me a hug. Though she smoked dope, Chicken was still a pretty thang to see. She looked just like Pam Grier and the drugs had not hurt her beauty one bit as of yet. She had only been smoking for a year, but so far so good.

"Scooby, tell me that you got a bump for me baby. Please tell me that you got something to wake me up." She batted her eyes and licked her succulent lips.

I tried to side step her to get into the house. She reached down and grabbed my hand. "Listen here soul man, you ain't gots to ignore me. I thought we was better than that." she hissed.

I yanked my arm away. "Slow down, Foxy momma. It ain't that type of party. You know I always got something for the crew. Baby, you just gotta hold tight and not play me so close."

"Yeah. Un huh. I got yo playing close, nigga. Now give me something to get right before you get in there and let Rallo's trifling ass smoke it all up. I need to wake up."

I slid her a twenty sack. She reached, cupped my dick and squeezed. "I'm gone get me some of this mule as soon as you quit playing games. I might be a dope fiend now, but I still got the tightest pussy in Chicago. Ask around Sugar. It ain't no secret. Don't let my hobbies fool you." She leaned and bit me on the neck before opening the door to their house. Rallo was just coming out of the bathroom. He had a can of air freshener spraying it into the air, holding his stomach. "Man, I don't know what I ate last night but something didn't agree with my stomach."

Chicken slumped down on the couch preparing her pipe. "It was probably all them damn white castle burgers you ate." She turned to me. "Scooby you should

43

have seen his ass last night, stuffing his face like he ain't have no damn sense. It was down right embarrassing." She started to flick her lighter on and off. Then, without getting it to flame she threw the lighter across the room. "Damn! One of y'all let me see your lighter."

Rallo came over to the couch and knelt down in front of her. "Damn, Chicken, where you get some candy from? Huh, let me see that pipe. I'll take a lil hit just to wake up, then you can get the rest." He tried to pry the pipe out of her hand.

She muffed him on the forehead and stood up. "Nigga you must be crazy. You got lungs like a semi truck. You can keep your lighter if you think I'm finna let yo' scurvy ass smoke up all my shit. Nigga please." She walked up to me and licked her thick lips. "Scooby, baby, let me see your lighter so I can take my medicine, obviously my man tripping." She rolled her eyes at Rallo.

Rallo mugged me as I handed it to her. Just to kill the damn drama, I threw him a twenty sack too. "Huh nigga, ain't no sense in you looking at me all crazy and shit. Gone head and get right so we can get out here and get some money." He nodded, then flamed away.

We walked into the Urban Apparel store on 95th and Carmen. I looked over at Rallo and saw that he was still geeking. His eyes were bucked, and his lips were drier than a peanut butter sandwich. He kept running his hand across his face. I scrunched my forehead growing irritated at his body language. *What the fuck is wrong with him?*

"Say, Blood, man you alright?" I whispered watching him closely

"Yea mane, I'm cool let's roll baby." His face sharpened up.

I touched the .38 special tucked inside my waist

Paid in Blood

band and waited for Chicken to come in and do her
thang.
Five minutes later, she walked in with a big stomach.
She was disguised as a pregnant woman. Me and Rallo
continued to cruise through the aisles like customers
ready for the purchase. The store specialized in Hip Hop
clothing. They had all the latest in Hip Hop fashions.
Today was Sunday, which meant that the Asian lady
would be working alone with her young daughter that
she was training. Her husband and son were busy
running the other store across 145th street. Everybody
went there after their church services. And the Asian
man was smart enough to have twenty percent off all
items on Sunday which brought out everybody because
the gear was tight.
   I had bussed a move two days ago where I caught
this young dude slipping. I could tell he was a rookie as
soon as I pulled up in the stolen station wagon. He ran
up to my car screaming "What you need dope head. I got
them boulders. Any size, all pure glass, so what you
looking for?" He said getting into the car.
   He couldn't have been no older than thirteen. I sized
him up quick and tucked my money back in my pocket
"Say, lil homie, I came over here to buy some dope
yesterday and somebody sold me some soap. How I
know that you ain't the one that did that?" My tone was
passive aggressive.
   "Yo, I don't get down like that. I'm a hustler, cuz. I
don't play games with nobody money, and I don't let
nobody play games with mine." He put on his best mug
and tried to look hard.
   "I can respect all that, lil homie, but the fact still
remains that some body got me for my shit. Now I'm a
hardworking man. I don't like for people to take
advantage of me just because I get high."

45

Hood Rich

He nodded. "Fa show."

"So, let me see what you working with, that way I know you keeping it on the up and up."

I watched as he went into his drawers and pulled out a Ziploc bag full of twenty-dollar rocks. They were so yellow they looked like cheese. I felt my mouth salivating. He opened the bag and handed me one. I took the rock and bit into it. The numbness raced into my gums immediately. He continued sitting in my passenger's seat watching me closely. After I confirmed that it was all good. I pulled at my dummy knot. I had a twenty-dollar bill on top with a hundred ones in the middle. "Let me get twenty of them. What kinda play you a give me if I buy twenty, shortie?"

He shook his head. "Nall, homie, this dope A-1. Ain't no deals jumping off, these twenties are really thirty pieces so you already getting over. You want twenty boulders, you gon' give me four hundred dollars or you ain't getting shit." He rested his hand on the bulge under his shirt, I couldn't do nothing but smile.

In one quick motion, I slammed the pointy part of my elbow into his temple, then grabbed the back of his head and slammed it into the dash board knocking him out cold. Then I drove down six blocks and pulled into the alley where I stripped him of his knot and the whole Ziploc bag of rocks. I even took the .38 special from out of his waist band and left his ass in the car.

After partying hard for two days, straight I was back low again. I was down to ten rocks and a few hundred dollars. This move had to go right with Chicken, or I was gone be back at surfing for another lick. That wasn't something I felt like doing. Plus, I had a feeling the lil chump I robbed was part of a bigger scheme.

Chicken waltzed into the store slow, pushing a stroller. She went right up to the front looking over some

Elie Saab dresses. The Asian lady was just making her way over to helping her when two other customers came into the store. A young dude about nineteen, and a female who had to be around the same age. You could tell that his intentions were to spend some cash on the fine light skinned girl that pranced around the place like she owned it. He looked back to me and Rallo and nodded. We nodded back and he put his attention back on the broad that he had come in with.

Damn, what the fuck is taking so long I was growing impatient. Just then, I heard a whole bunch of liquid hitting the floor. Then I heard Chicken scream out. "Oh my god, my water just broke."

The Asian lady ran around the counter to help her along with her daughter. Right away me and Rallo pulled the bags out of our drawers and began stuffing them with Vera Wang, Eli Saab, Alexander McQueen, Prada, Gucci and Dolce and Gabbana dresses. We filled up two bags a piece, slipped out the store and came back with two more bags and filled them up too.

Meanwhile, Chicken was hollering and screaming like she was dying. Every time the Asian lady or her daughter tried to leave her side, she held on to them, so they were never able to call an ambulance. After me and Rallo made three trips we volunteered to take her to the hospital and the Asian lady quickly agreed, even gave me a fifty-dollar bill for my troubles. We threw Chicken's ass into the car and loaded up the stroller, then sped away from the scene laughing hysterically.

Hood Rich

Chapter 6
Scooby

After we sold all that shit it was time to party. I was happy as a muthafucka that things went as smoothly as they did. I knew that going back to that store would be out of the question, but I just didn't give a fuck. I was just thankful that we got up out of there without having to up that burner. Going down for the theft was never as bad as going down for armed robbery and that's definitely what was going to take place next had the fake in labor gig not have worked. But it had and I was ecstatic.

I bought me two ounces for my trouble. I wasn't planning on sharing my shit with Chicken or Rallo either, they had already gotten their cut of the money, so whatever they did was on them, I just didn't give a fuck. My head was hurting. I knew that a migraine would be setting in soon, so I wanted to take me a few blasts before that happened.

Damn, I felt good. My heart was beating fast, I was on cloud nine, and I didn't have a care in the world. Yea, this was living. I heard a knock at the back door snapping me out of my zone. I grabbed my .38 special off of the table and asked, "Who is it?"

"Scooby, it's Amanda from upstairs, I need to use your phone because I lost my cell phone and I ain't got no home phone."

I opened the door immediately. Amanda was fine as a muthafucka let me tell you. She was about twenty-two years old, slim with a real athletic figure. She was burnt caramel and had the prettiest dimples. Her man had been locked down for two years and fro what I knew she had been holding him down strong. I ain't never see no niggas running in and out of her crib. I also knew that they had two little boys, one was just three years old. Amanda was on her own and surviving. When I opened the door, she stood in the hallway in some real tight biker shorts that left very little to the imagination. She had on a tank top with a bra on underneath. I couldn't keep my eyes from roaming all over her body, even her toes were perfect. This lil minx was hot.

"Come on in baby girl and make yourself at home." I looked around; the place wasn't too dirty. Even though I smoke crack, I always keep my crib nice and I stay dressed fresh. I ain't the average fien, I still had a few principles left and self respect.

"Thank you, Scooby." I saw her eyes land on the table where the two ounces were on top of a plate. She turned to me and shook her head. "I see I caught you at a bad time."

"Nall, you straight. I was just in the middle of taking care of some business. What, you never seen dope before or something?"

She looked at me like I was the lamest comedian in the world, then placed her hand on her small hip.

"Now, you know that's the stupidest question in the world. That's all I've been around my whole life is that stuff. My momma smoked, my daddy smoked, my baby daddy tooted, and sold the shit and that's what he got locked up for. Two years to go, so yeah, I am more than familiar with that shit."

"Okay, calm down, lil momma. The phone is right there on the table in the dining room, do whatever you need to do."

I watched her walk off with those shorts hugging her every curve. Her hips moved with a natural sway. Her perfume left a trail behind her and before I knew what was going on, my dick was standing straight up against my stomach throbbing. She was a fox, and the more I watched her, the more I knew that I had to have her, or if I couldn't have her, I had to have a taste of her. Here I was, a forty-six-year-old man, lusting for a woman damn near half of my age, and I really do mean lusting too. I bet she ain't had nobody that a eat that pussy like I would. I would eat that pussy and toss that back door with no problem. That girl was meant to be made love to.

I watched the way she carelessly left her legs spread as she talked on the phone. I saw how her thighs glistened. They must have been freshly oiled. She must have sensed me looking up at her because we locked eyes and she smiled and started to rub her thigh with her right hand. *Was she purposely seducing me? I* couldn't tell, but I knew that I liked it.

After her phone call, she thanked me by giving me a hug. "You know I appreciate that, and I owe you one."

Damn, she smelled so good. This girl was driving me crazy. "Aww baby it ain't no thang. Anytime you need to use the phone just let me know, or if you need me for anything else you let me know about that too.

There I'd said it; I'd put that out there. I knew she was smart enough to pick up on my vibe. I was praying that she took the bait. I was willing to give her whatever it took to get a shot at that ass, and I do mean whatever it took.

"Well I'm good for now." she smiled. "But you know what, I'ma do some thing for you I bet you ain't ate nothing all day long have you?" She looked me up and down sizing me up. "When was the last time you had a home cooked meal? I'm always seeing you with restaurant bags, and I don't ever smell no cooking aromas coming from down here. So how long has it been?"

I was kinda embarrassed to even tell the truth, because the truth was that I couldn't remember the last time that I actually had a home cooked meal. I had eaten restaurant food for at least the last year and beyond that my memory was kind of shaky. "You know what sweetheart; I can't even remember the last time I had a real live home cooked meal. Seem like it been ages."

"That's what I thought. So, I'm going to go upstairs and finish cooking, then I'm gone bring you down a plate and we gon' start putting some meat on them bones." She paused looking me over. "You know what, you would be a fine older man if you had some meat on you. You're obviously cute and got the height. You're just way too skinny, but I can help you with that." She smiled. "Tonight, I'ma whip you up something real good."

I knew she was talking about food, but my dick was rock hard and her words to me were mesmerizing.

Ten minutes after she left my house, Rallo came beating on my front door like a deranged maniac. I opened it and he flew past me into the living room holding an ice pack up to his jaw. I glared at him like he had lost his damn mind.

"Blood what's the matter with you? You look like you done fucked around and got into some bullshit, what happened?"

He continued to pace back and forth like he was losing his mind. I really didn't feel like being apart of the bullshit tonight. I had my mind set on how I was going to seduce that pretty young thang. It was just like Rallo to run his crazy ass into the spot bringing with him a whole bunch of drama. I could only imagine what was going on.

"Them muthafuckas jumped me Scooby, for no

reason. Just ran up on me and started swinging." He continued pacing back and forth. "I never so much as said a word to the young niggas. They just walked up to me and started tearing into my ass."

Even though I ain't want to get in the middle of Rallo's bullshit, I wanted to get a better understanding as to what he was talking about. I was completely against young niggas that thought it was cool to whoop on dope fiends just because they were addicts. If that was the case, I was gon' tear into some ass tonight real lovely.

"Rallo, why do you think they jumped on you? Do you think it is because you are an addict, or have you done something to them in the past that you may have forgotten about?" I looked him up and down real closely trying to detect any traces of him maybe bringing this ass whooping on himself, but I detected none. The more he spoke the more I knew that he was telling the truth, he had been targeted because he was a crack addict, and that to me simply wasn't a good enough reason for somebody to be putting their hands on my partner. That could have very well been me, and the thought of me being on that receiving end is completely unacceptable.

We pulled up and parked three houses down form the young kats that had jumped on Rallo. The neighborhood was kinda quiet which was a good and bad thing. Good because there weren't many people out, but bad because I intended on making a whole lot of noise. I felt my eye beginning to twitch and that usually meant that it was time for murder.

"Is that them niggaz right there?" I slid my black leather gloves on pulling the ski mask down over my face watching Rallo do the same thing. I was ready to get the show on the road. I was anxious.

He nodded. "Yep, that's every last one of them

young niggaz. Blood, I swear I'm finna try to hit all six of they ass at least twice. He slapped the clip in the mach 11, holding it with a red bandana.

We watched them for a lil while longer, then Rallo got out the car and made his way down the alley. I started the engine and pulled the car directly in front of their complex but across the street. I felt my heart beating faster and that salty taste come into my mouth. As soon as I saw Rallo making his way on the side of their house I stepped out the car. One of the younger lil niggas hollered out "Yo, cuz its a hit." Then they all turned to look at me, but it was too late. Rallo ran full speed and began airing the porch out. *Blaaat! Blaaaaat!* They started tripping over each other as the bullets tore into their young fleshes. Some that almost got away I finished off. *Blocka! Blocka!* Straight head shots. Rallo ran over the fallen victims emptying his entire clip, then one by one we went through their pockets and took whatever they had on them which wasn't much. But this wasn't about the money, this was about the principle. One victim was still kicking, body struggling to survive the gun play. I shot him twice in the back of the dome, then flipped him over and almost threw up. I had killed a fucking girl. Why was she out here? Why did she have a hood on as if she was one of the boys. *Fuck, what have I done?* I started to panic.

We jumped into the car and smashed. Back at my crib, after setting the stolen whip on fire, I was beside myself. How the fuck had we killed a little girl, she had to be about fourteen. Where the fuck were her parents? What the fuck do we do now? I felt like screaming.

"Man calm down, Joe, it ain't our fault. The lil bitch had herself disguised so she became a casualty of war. Fuck it! Shit happens."

I spun on the balls of my feet and looked him over

and I swear in that moment I wanted to kill his ass. "Muthafucka, don't you understand that we just killed a lil girl? That that li'l girl ain't have nothing to do with you getting jumped. That the only reason she was out there was because her hormones was probably getting the best of her. Now you sitting here like killing that baby ain't no big deal. Nigga, have you lost your muthafucking mind?" I was heated.

Rallo must have sensed that because he didn't say nothing for a long moment. "Look, Scooby, all I'm saying is that that shit over and done with. We can't change what happened, so we might as well keep on trucking baby. You feel me?"

Ambulances and fire trucks were screaming in the background reminding me of my mistake. We had murdered seven shorties just six blocks away. What the fuck was I thinking? It had to be this crack that was getting the best of me. Damn, I gotta leave this shit alone. This shit fucking me up.

Hood Rich

Chapter 7
Roman

I was sitting in the crib playing chess by myself when I heard a loud banging on the door. The first thing I thought about was the law. Shit! I started tucking guns and hiding shit to the best of my abilities. How the fuck did they find me already, I wondered? The beating intensified and my heart beat intensified with it. Man, fuck, this they gone have to kill me! I ain't going back to prison for no mufucka. I ran in my room and flipped the bed grabbing my AK-47, slapping a fifty-round magazine in it. Fuck it, I'ma hold court right here tonight, fuck prison. I ran back into the front room of the apartment.

"Who is it?" If I heard any kind of walkie talkie or police response, I was prepared to start shooting through the door. I had four more magazines around my waist ready for the reload, so I was taking at least ten mufuckas with me.

"Baby, its Rihanna, please open the door. I need you so bad right now, they just killed my little sister." She slumped down on the floor in front of my door and began crying her lil eyes out.

After I pulled her inside, she sat on the couch telling me everything that had happened. She said that her lil sister Do had been down at their cousin's house spending some time with him when they were bum rushed and massacred. Do, had been shot more than eight times including twice to the back of the head, execution style. She continued to break down, her breathing coming in gasps.

I wrapped my arms around her protectively. Rihanna was really the only female outside of my sisters that I cared about, well her and our daughter. You see, Rihanna was my daughter's mother and although we were not together, she and I still maintained a strong bond. Her sister, Do, was my lil heart as well.

I had just bought her a couple outfits a few days ago, now she was gone. I can't imagine what could have happened in her life of karma that would make such a horrific death be justified. I didn't know what to say.

Rihanna cried into my shoulder, squeezing me with all of her might, I knew that D was her heart. After their mother got killed, she had been raising her on her own and for the most part she had did a terrific job, until now. I didn't know how to comfort her because I was still emotionally dead from losing my own mother. I wasn't emotionally ready to help somebody else heal. As much as I cared about her and her sister Do, at that moment, I didn't feel any compassion to her murder. I don't know what that meant, but I knew I would have to fake my compassion, after all this was my daughter's mother and I did care about her a great deal. "Babe, calm down. It's gone be alright, just tell me what you want me to do and I got you. You know we gotta be strong for each other. You been holding me down all through my pains with my mom's being gone, so I got you boo." I tilted her chin upward and looked deep into her eyes. "You hear me? Anything you need, I got you."

I watched her wipe the tears from her cheeks then get up. She was silent for a long while as she paced back and forth in front of me. "Roman, you know that I try and do everything right in life. I try to respect everybody, and I try my best to follow all of the rules of society. I pay my bills on time and pay the government their taxes. I try and cross all of my tees, and dot all of my i's. But it seems like no matter how hard I try to do the right things; bad things just keep happening to either me or my family. I am so sick of playing by the rules and getting fucked left and right."

She balled up her small fist and began smashing it into the palm of her hand over and over. "That was my baby sister. I was responsible for her and I failed her. I failed her and my mother." Tears began pouring from her eyes again, her nose began to run. "Baby I want you to find the nigga that did this shit to D. and I want you to kill his ass a thousand times. Or betta yet, I want you to let me kill his ass in honor of my sister. I done played the sanctified and filled with the holy ghost role. I'm ready to fight society back the same way they're fighting me! Now for a long time I have known what you do out here in these streets and it never bothered me because I love you so fucking much. But, now baby I am depending on you to find the niggas that did this and to make they ass pay for killing my baby sister for nothing." She turned to me with pleading eyes. "Will you help me, boo?"

Right then, I was feeling the utmost sympathy for her I started remembering how she held me down for the seven years I was down. I thought about when they were threatening me with life and threatening to give her fifty years for harboring a fugitive, she never buckled. I remembered the way how she held her head up and brought my daughter to see me every month, twice a month, and the drive was five hours away from Chicago. I remembered all the times she caught me cheating and how she never could break away from a nigga, even though at those times she hated me. When I got shot five times, she stayed in the hospital with me for three months straight and at that time we were only kids of seventeen. Every day after school she rushed out to be by my side at the hospital. This girl loved my dirty drawers. After all of the sacrifices she had made for me

I would have no problem making this one for her. Especially since I was imagining my daughter being with D when she got gunned down. My daughter could have very well been a victim as well and since that was a definite possibility, I began imagining that it was actually the case and I started to get angry. My heart started beating faster.

By the time I had made my mind up she was kneeling in front of me begging for me to see things her way. "Baby say something, you've been quiet for damn near ten minutes. Are you mad at me? Was I wrong for asking you what I did? Say something." I shook my head. "N'all, you straight boo. You earned the right to ask me that question. My answer is yes. No doubt. I got you. Let me see what the streets talking about. As soon as I find out who changed your lil sister, I'ma take care of that. Nall, matter fact, I'mma bring them to you and we gone take care of that shit together. You game for that?"

Her eye lids lowered, then she nodded her head. I felt her hands on my legs begin to shake. "Don't worry boo, I'ma handle the big part, let me do what I do okay?" I leaned down and kissed her on the forehead. Her being in front of me on her knees was causing my manhood to stir, but I knew that she was grieving, otherwise, I would have had her swallowing me whole already. I ain't never met nobody better that my baby mother on the head. Maybe she just knew my body, either way, she was the coldest.

I slipped out the crib early in the morning, right after Rihanna went to work. It was about seven and I was headed to my lil homie's crib to wake her ass up. When I got there, I beat on the door until she answered it with two chrome .45s in her hands.

"Nigga, on my blood, I swear to God if this wasn't

you standing on my porch, I was finna kill whoever else would have been. Why the fuck you beating on the door like the muthafucking police?" She stepped to the side and I walked past her still laughing. She slammed the door. "I'm glad you find this shit funny, because I don't." She put one gun in her waistband and the other one on the living room table. I watched as she picked up a stuffed Cuban cigar and lit it. I immediately smelled the gas that my father smoked. She coughed a few times then handed the cigar to me. I took a few tokes, tried to resist coughing, failed, then passed it back to her. The high took over right away. I knew this shit had to come from my old man because it was top of the line.

"Shortie, let me get a juice or somethin, that shit got my mouth dry as hell already." I ran my tongue across my lips to moisten them.

When she came back, she handed me a Snapple. I wasn't a fan of that brand because I knew Snapple was alleged to have been responsible for funding the Klu Klux Klan for years, I turned that pink lemonade up and killed the whole bottle anyway.

"So, what brings you over here this early in the morning?" She was sitting across from me on the love seat while I sat on the couch watching her lil pretty ass smoking a Newport short. Though Binkey was fine as a muthafucka, she didn't fuck with niggas at all. That was fucked up because she was a carbon copy of Megan Good. Her body was immaculate, her lips were so thick that you could tell that she used to suck her thumb. Even though she was beautiful, Binkey was as crazy of a killer as I was, if not more insane. Her father had molested her from the time she was eight until she killed him at fifteen. The entire while she was going through the drama with him, we were best friends. I had known her ever since we were six years old. She was my first crush and I was hers.

"It's fucked up that I need a reason to shoot over and see my peeps. What? I can't miss you or something and just be wanting to see you?" I gave her a look like I was hurt.

"Nigga, please. Miss me with that bullshit. You got a phone, and I know damn well that if you ain't have some real shit on your mind that your ass would not be here right now. So, miss a bitch with that bullshit 'fore I get up and whoop yo tall ass."

I laughed at that. My eyes trailed down and looked right between her legs. Her night gown had raised, and I could see her red panties. My dick instantly got hard, so I reached in my pants and pulled my dick up towards my stomach so it could breath. She must have noticed what I was doing because she smiled.

"Damn boy, your ass is so freaky. What, me wearing this lil gown is turning you on that much?" She looked down, then spread her legs some more making the gown get lost in her lap. Her pussy's indentation was molded into her panties. She took two fingers and rubbed them on her crotch's front until her sex lips had the panties trapped. She looked up at me seductively. "Do this turn you on, Roman?"

I'd pulled my dick out by this time and was openly stroking it in front of her while she rubbed on the front of her panties. When she stuffed the panties all the way into her pussy so that the lips appeared on each side, my hand was jerking my shit so fast I was almost in a frenzy. Then, she turned around and showed me her ass while pulling her thong tightly between her globes. I came, my juices shooting two feet in front of me and all over my hand. Binkey never ceased to amaze me, she was the only woman who had that effect on me. There was something about her that captivated and turned me on at the same time. Even though she was my nigga, I never forgot that she was also a woman, and she never forgot that I was a man.

"Roman, come here before you clean yourself off." I walked over to her with my pants still down. I was semi hard, and my dick was leaking from my climax. As soon as I got in front of her she grabbed it and squeezed it. The gel came to the tip of my head, she swiped that with her tongue and smacked her hand deep inside her panties. I caught slight glimpses of her fat lips, her pussy was bald as she worked three fingers into herself and slurped on my dirty dick.

The more her head jerked forward, the lower the strap on her night gown descended until her left breast was exposed show casing a thick brown nipple that stood at attention. I reached out and pinched it and she slapped my hand. "You know the rules, no touching, this is me-time." Binkey began moaning to herself, then she screamed out and I saw her squirting all over her fingers before she sucked them clean, I came seconds after seeing her swallowing my gifts.

"Alright, now that we got that out of the way, lets get down to business. We had both showered and were facing each other smoking on a Cuban. After releasing a nut my mind always cleared. I was able to think more thoroughly, and I seemed to feel a bit more relaxed. Now I was getting angry all over again. I was getting into that mind frame.

"Sis, the reason I came over here so early is because some niggaz killed Rihanna's lil sister two days ago."

"What, who you talking about, li'l D?" She stood up ready to blow.

"Yep, they shot her eight times. Twice in the back of the head while she was laying face down." I still couldn't believe that fact. She was only fourteen years old, whoever killed her was enacting some kind of revenge, I thought to myself.

"Damn, that's fucked up. When is her funeral? I'mma have to go and pay my respects." She whispered with her head down.

"It's Sunday, but you already know that I don't do no churches so I won't be there, so you can give her my love for me."

Binkey shook her head. "You sure this shit ain't got nothing to do with Pouchie nem' being knocked off?"

I had told her about the Pouchie and Y-Ketta hit because she was my ace and me and her ain't keep nothing business wise away from each other. Me and this girl had shed blood together. We held no secrets period. I trusted her more than anybody else breathing.

"Nall, I don't think so because if it did why would they wet up my baby momma's sister and not hit her or my daughter?" I began   mulling that shit over in my head. "Wait a minute, I did just take shorty shopping the day before she got changed over. And we were riding through that hood in my truck together. I saw Moe and Tim that same day and them niggaz gave me one of them knowing ass looks, they knew what was good. When I nodded whud up to Moe, that nigga ain't even nod back."

Binkey was already loading up her tech .9 "So what you saying, we gotta go pay them niggas a visit?"

Chapter 8
Seven

I'm already knowing this nigga can't hold me. How they gone put a white boy on me with the game on the line, especially when I'm hot. I had thirty-eight points and was six for six from three-point land. The score was tied at one hundred six a piece and the clock was winding down, it was bit at sixteen seconds, and we were already in overtime. Our point guard passed the ball in to me at half court. I dribbled and planted my back into the chest of Ohio State's best pure defender. We were playing for the Big Ten championship and the game was on the line, and the team was on my back. They doubled me at half but with my dribbles I easily split the defenders leaving them behind me. I scowered the floor looking for an open man. I saw our center, but he was known for tricking off easy buckets, plus this wasn't the time to be taking no gambles. I read the clock again it was now at eight seconds and counting. I thought about pulling up for a short jumper, but they knew that was my strong suit, so I faked as if I was gonna stop and pop which drew their center. I spun around him and as the clock hit two seconds, I jumped and dunked the ball hard in the face of their power forward just as the clock expired, giving us the lead and the win! The crowd went insane, everybody rushed me and held me in the air. We were the Big Ten Champions and all I could do was think about my mother.

Chapter 9
Tarig

"Blood, I don't care what you niggas talking about. If anybody finna holler at my nigga, that shit finna be one on one, or we can send this bitch to the moon, so what's it gone be?" We were standing in the laundry center. I had Peety behind me. In front of me was ten studs who thought they was finna put they hands on my homie, because he had knocked out one of they niggas that morning in the shower. See, ma'fuckas thought that since the homie was skinny and goofy, t he was a coward or something. What they failed to realize was that he was a goon. My nigga was about whatever action the next nigga was about. I didn't give a fuck what these niggas was screaming. I was prepared to leave a few niggas leaking over my mans.

One of the stockier niggas spoke up. "Look, Ankh, we ain't got no problem with you, but that nigga gotta answer for his sins. He done knocked out one of the folds, so it's a must he be held accountable."

I seriously hated niggas that tried to hide behind Islam. Here was this big, goofy ass nigga with a sweated-out perm in his head screaming Ankh. I ain't never seen this stud in Juma'h or Taleem before. He never salaamed any of the brothas, but now all the sudden when the heat is on, he hollering Ankh. Fuck this nigga!

"Say, homie, which one of you niggas finna fight my homie head up? Y'all can miss me with that jumping shit. You niggaz betta make y'all mind up and quick or else I'ma get the Muslims involved, for real." The big nigga with the perm looked at me like I had offended him. I saw his face frown up and I just lost it. I swung and hit him so hard I felt his nose crack instantly. I caught him two more times while he was falling, knocked out cold. I sliced his mans across the face who was standing next to him, just as I saw Peety slam one nigga on his head and knock out another one. Two cowards ran and one stud swung and caught me in the eye. I grabbed his arm, twisted it then slammed it on top of my shoulder breaking it, flipped him over my back then stomped him six times in the face. Peety was caught in this funky, fat nigga's bear hug, I came from behind and kicked him in the nuts, he dropped Peety right away and we whooped his ass until he was a bloody mess. We left then in the laundry corridor leaking.

Back in the cell, I was nervous as hell. It felt good to finally get some action, but now I had to worry about them white folks and I knew they played a dirty game. I was trying my best to get into that pre-release program. I started thinking about my son and being home with him and his mother. I hoped that these niggas played the tough role, but as soon as you got into their ass the real bitch seemed to come out of them. Finding a real gangsta was rare, especially in prison now a days.

Peety was laid back eating a bag of Doritos like he didn't have a care in the world. I had to laugh at the homie because no matter what, he never seemed to lose his composure. He was trying to get into the same program as me, but that never stopped him from cutting into a nigga's ass. The more I was around him, the more I began to respect him.

It was quiet for a whole week. The police hadn't come to us and said anything so we figured that the studs had kept their mouths closed. That meant that they had every intention of coming back at us, which was fine with me. I was never the one to duck action. I was pretty good with my hands, and if they wanted knife play, that shit didn't concern me either. I believed in predestination, which meant that whatever was supposed to happen would happen. There was no way to out run fate, but you better believe that I was gonna be ready for it. Don't let my belief in predestination allow you to think that I was careless, nall, never that.

"Ankh, word is that the Harper South boys got a hit out on you and yo mans. They talking about they putting up five thousand to the first nigga that take one of y'all out, that means it's ten total, or five a piece."

I continued my set on the bench press, hitting the bar to my chest then straightening my arms all the way out, repeating the process, doing sets of fifteen. I had heard about that hit, and if you asked me, all that that meant was those niggaz was cowards and couldn't carry out their own business. That did put a huge target on my head right along with Peety's, so I would have to watch my back and his. All it took was for a random nigga to come up and stab us the fuck up. I was worried, but at the same time I was prepared for whatever them niggas had in mind. Real niggas don't approach war with a worried heart, your shit had to be cold. You had to be ready for any outcome. I ain't never been no coward or pussy. The fact that these Harper Building niggaz were putting money up on my head meant that they feared me, and they feared the homie, Peety. Right then and there, I knew that I wasn't finna wait for them niggas to have somebody come at me. I was finna go at their asses first and get some blood on my hands. Fuck it, this what it is!

"Yeah, Anki, I heard about that lil bounty. I guess them niggas can't stand to take an ass whoopin'."

Wazire was one of the older Muslim brothers, he had been down for twenty years already and was one of the institutions respected Imams. He was about six foot three, weighing in at three hundred plus pounds of solid muscle. He was on the ground counting down from a hundred diamond push-ups. When he finished, he dusted his hands off and continued to spot me. I replaced the bar and stood up.

"Ankh, I don't know what you got yourself into, but you know that you are under this fold of Islam. You're apart of this Umm'at (Community) so if them Harper boys is waging war against you, then they waging war against all of us Muslims. Do you understand that?"

He ran his fingers through his big beard, sweat pouring from his bald head. He looked me directly in the eyes and frowned. I thought about what he had said for a minute, then immediately waved that off. The last thing I wanted to do was get the Umma't involved in a war that I was certain I could take care of myself. You see, once the Muslims get involved, they conduct a full investigation and before you know it you find yourself getting chastised for some shit that ain't have nothing to do with why they were aiding you. So, I knew right away that I wasn't gone let them aid me. I was selling narcotics and shit. I knew if they found out about that, I would have some serious problems on my hands. So, I slapped my hand on his big ass shoulder and shook my head. "Look I appreciate the gesture, Anki, but I got into this on my own. This is something that developed while I was in a state of slumber. This had nothing to do with the Umma't. I will be sure to crush these kaffirs so that I can get back on my deen. I got this though, Ankh, make sure you let the brothers know not to intervene."

I found Peety in the cell sharpening his blade and eating a bag of Doritos at the same time. His eyes were focused on the task at hand, but at the same time they seemed distant. He was mumbling to himself and his upper lip kept curling on the right side.

"Whut up, Joe, you good?"

He nodded his head without verbalizing he was cool. "Peety fuck this bullshit, we finna go holla at them niggas as soon as rec let out. I ain't finna sit around and let them niggas bring me no drama. I'm finna go at these niggas chin, and that's all there is to it."

He kept nodding his head. "Tarig, I'm ready to kill somethin, blood. I'm tired of everybody fucking with me because I'm all alone in this muthafucka. Since these niggas wanna put money upon my head, I'm gone try and take one of theirs off. I'm done with all the games, bro. Fuck these niggas!"

I felt the homie one hundred percent. I saw where he wanted to take shit and I was with it. Fuck it! The niggas obviously wanted us knocked off or else they wouldn't be putting up ten gees on our heads, but it was one thing I had to know before we took it there. I had to know what had made Peety knock one of the niggas out in the shower in the first place, so I asked him exactly that question.

"Man, joe, I'mma be honest with you. I bought some powder from that nigga, Groovy, for thirty dollars. When I got back to the cell to do my thang, I found out that that shit was barely ten percent. The nigga had sold me some crushed pills, so I went and hollered at him about it while he was getting into the shower. The nigga got to talking real slick and real disrespectful, calling me all kinds of dope feens, treating me like less than a man. I looked around and saw that everybody was looking at me snickering, so by the time the nigga got around to calling me a bitch, I had knocked him out. You know I don't do the bitch word, Tarig. Niggas gone respect my gangsta, one way or another. Ain't no bitch in my blood."

I nodded, and I was really with the homie after that. "Peep, joe this what we gone do."

71

Hood Rich

Paid in Blood

Chapter 10
Binkey

"Damn, shortie, you thick as a muthafucka. You fine as hell. What's really good? Holla at ya boy."

"Nall, fuck that, holla at me! Where you from? What's it gone take for a nigga to get a piece of that ass tonight?"

I stopped in my tracks, sizing Moe and Tim up. I knew them niggas wasn't gone be able to resist these tight ass Jordache jeans. That's one weakness I knew I would forever be able to use against most men. Their weakness for a sexy body, it was the that single thing that every man would never be able to get out of his system. I was walking my lil poodle, Yarnie, and them niggaz was on the side of their house shooting dice with two other hustlers. I really ain't care who the other two was. I watched as Tim and Moe stepped away from the dice game just as two more men filled their spots where they had been on one knee. They both came and stood in front of me, looking me up and down as if I was their last meal. They both had a wad of money in their hands, obviously trying to show off in front of me, which was typical. Tim reached out and grabbed my arm.

"Say, lil momma, you look familiar as hell, where do I know you from?" He smiled that smile that I am sure many woman could not refuse. He was quite handsome, deep waves, brown eyes, and a lil baby face. Whereas, Moe was dark skinned, with a nappy fro, he was also kind of handsome. But I was familiar with their type. They only saw me as the meat in their sandwich. Neither of these dudes had have no respect for me or no other woman. In their mind I was a bitch, a whore, garbage. To them I wasn't worthy to be respected. They saw me as stupid, an average hood rat that laid on her back just

73

to be down with them, so that's the role I played for their asses.

"Damn I see y'all out here having money. How can a bitch get a piece of the pie?"

Moe smiled and licked his lips. "I'm saying shortie, all you gotta do is be down for the cause. Mafucka's a definitely take care of you and make sure you get straight. With a body like that, you better believe that you worthy to be down with the team."

Tim jumped in. "What you doing tonight, you wanna come fuck with us on some real shit? We can pop a few bottles and trick a few dollars. What would you say to that, baby girl?"

As soon as that nigga called me baby girl I got vexed and started thinking about my father. I started having flash backs of the molestation and I knew that I was going to enjoy killing Tim. That nigga was caramel colored just like my punk ass daddy. Even though my heart started beating fast, I knew that I had to calm down. So, I took a deep breath and smiled batting my eye lashes.

"I mean I strip a lil bit, so if you saying you want me to be y'all's private dancer tonight then I'm game, but I ain't cheap though.

Tim pulled out a thick knot, all hundreds. "Shortie, name yo price, just promise me I'mma get to hit this," He grabbed my ass and it took every ounce of restraint in me not to blow his head off right then and there. I was seriously imagining him laying in a casket with multiple gun shot wounds to his face. Niggas always thought they could just grab on you. I hated that shit more than anything. Now, I was gone kill this nigga, too. Roman was gone just have to be mad at me.

"I promise boo. What time y'all want me to meet y'all back here?"

I knew that this was their safe house. I fucked with a few bitches that were familiar with these two cheeps. So, I wanted to get their asses in there, that way we could also capitalize off of whacking them. Roman was just out for blood, but I was always thinking about my paper. No matter what, that was first and for most. Yarnie lifted up her back leg and pissed right on Tim's Jordans. I couldn't help but laugh, until he made a move like he wanted to stomp my dog. That's when I pushed him away from her and almost lost my cool.

"Calm down baby, I know them ain't your only pair of Jordans with all that money you having. We sorry, she just didn't know no better." I reached out and grabbed his dick. "Don't kill the good thing we got going."

He smiled, then we made arrangements for later that night.

Hood Rich

Chapter 11
Roman

I was posted in the bushes in the gangway for two straight hours before Binkey finally came and opened the bathroom window. It was the same window that pointed out to the gangway, and it was the window that we had decided she would open in order for me to climb in. When I saw her, I came out of the shadows and handed her the machete' and her .45 automatic. She said to give her ten minutes before I broke in. I nodded.

I pulled my mask down and allowed the time to elapse. Then, I reached up and climbed into the window, landing right in a bath tub. As soon as I got in there, I smelled heavy weed smoke. They were playing that R. Kelly "*Strip for You*". The bathroom door was closed, so I slowly opened it, peeking out to see what was good. The bathroom door opened right into a short hallway, that ran directly into the living room. All the lights were off, which was perfect. I cocked the .40 and twisted on the silencer my Pops had given me for my birthday that year. He gave me silencers and noise reductions for each one of my fire arms. My Pops just knew what kind of nigga I was, and I appreciated that.

I stayed low to the floor following the music, when I got to the living room, I could not believe my eyes. The room was decorated by candles which really set the tone. Tim and Moe were sitting back on the couch while, and this is what I couldn't believe, Binkey danced in the middle of the floor so seductively that for a moment I got caught up in the show. She wound her body like a snake, clad in only a red thong and matching see through bra. She turned around with her back to them and made her ass clap before hitting the splits and bouncing up and down. Then, she was on all fours popping her pussy causing the material to wedge itself between her lips. I was so hard and mesmerized I had to snap out of that shit before I lost my bearings on the situation.

I ran up to the couch and smashed the handle of my gun into the back of Tim's head and whipped the wire around Moe's neck in one quick motion. Tim fell off the couch and Binkey kicked him right in the chin, knocking him out instantly. Moe tried to pull the wire from around his neck with no success.

"Punk, stop struggling before I kill yo ass. Nigga put your hands down or I'mma choke yo ass to death. "He complied.

After we tied them up, I interrogated them about lil shorty D. "Say, one of you niggas know what happened to them shorties that got gunned down last week. I advise somebody to speak up, or its gon' be two more dead bodies on this block. Now, one of them kids was a little girl and she was like my lil sister. Somebody shot her eight times for no reason. Somebody better tell me something, speak up!" I looked back and forth between the two men. By this time, Tim was woke and Binkey was back dressed. They both remained silent. I looked at Binkey, "Do your thang ma, these niggas think its a game."

She jumped up and stuffed a rag into Tim's mouth. Then she produced her machete', swiped, and sliced his ear off and tossed it on to his lap. When he saw his ear, that nigga's eyes got so big, all I heard was him screaming. Binkey laughed and sliced his other ear off and this time threw it on Moe's lap. Before he could start hollering, I pressed the .40 Glock to his forehead.

"Nigga, you bet not start screaming, now who the fuck killed my lil sister? You niggaz run this block, somebody know something."

"Man, I don't know who, bucked them shorties, joe,

me and the homie was trying to figure that shit out ourselves. I swear to God, I don't know. I -"

Binkey stuffed a rag into his mouth, then sliced off the tip of his nose, then a chunk off each one of his cheeks. I pulled the gag out of Tim's mouth, while Moe screamed into the rag.

"Listen bro, we been beefing with them niggaz in Englewood. They came through here spraying two days before that, they must have come back and wet the block up again. They want this turf over here, saying we clocking too much money."

"Who is the niggaz? Give me some names." I demanded!

"Moeshe and J.J, they calling shots for them niggas over there, they been sending lil shorties over here to wet the block. Your lil sister must have gotten caught in the cross fire, that shit ain't got nothing to do with us."

Binkey stuffed the rag back into his mouth, walked behind him and cut his right hand off and tossed it on to his lap. "Bitch nigga, that's for grabbing my ass."

He was screaming into the rag and I couldn't help laughing. That was the reason I loved this girl so much. I swear, one day I was gone marry her ass. Wasn't nobody else more perfect for me than she was. I turned to Moe and shook my head. I pressed the .40 to Tim's forehead, telling him to stop all that fucking screaming, then I took the gag out of Moe's mouth.

"How much money y'all got in this Ma'fucka? We ain't looking to kill nobody, all we want is the dope and money, then you niggas can go. So, where the shit at and how much?"

Moe was silently weighing his options. He saw Binkey walking toward him with the rag and started to spill his guys. "We got two bricks in the pantry and a hundred and fifty thousand in the deep freezer. I got ten gees in my drawers, and that nigga got ten gees in his. I'll show y'all where everything at, just please keep that crazy bitch away from me with that blade."

I ran all over the house following his directions. When everything was recovered and bagged in pillow cases, I let Binkey do her thang. Watching this part always made me hard for her.

She took her machete and stood in front of Moe first, she walked around him in circles and stopped right in front of him again. I was wondering what she was doing, and I got my answer quick. She was staring him right in the eyes, respecting the rule of *always look a man in the eyes before you kill him.* In one slick motion, she whipped her arm through the air and began slicing, first his face then his chest and finally she was behind him trailing the blade from one ear to the next. After she killed him, she stuck her hand inside his open mouth and cut his tongue out, tossing it on his lap.

"That's for snitching and giving up your stashes so easily." she growled with a look of disgust. I knew she hated snitches. She had lost her brother when eight members out of his crew snitched on him. They gave him life in the feds under the R.I.C.O. Act.

Before she could get to Tim, I pressed the barrel of my .40 to his forehead and squeezed the trigger twice, splattering the back wall with his brain fragments. Binkey looked at me as if she was completely pissed off. I didn't care, we had already spent too much time on this job. I grabbed the pillow cases and we jetted.

Back at her crib, she was livid. We had stopped at Hodari's Barbeque. After she re-warmed the food up in the microwave, Binky sat it in front of me without saying a word, then she sat on the couch leaving a nice distance between us. I could tell she was giving me the cold shoulder and I was thinking about ignoring her ass, but I couldn't. There was something about her that just drove me crazy. She was the only female breathing that got me so weak over her ass. "So, what, you ain't fucking with me now?"

She curled up the right side of her face. "Boy, ain't nobody thinking about you. You betta eat your food before it gets cold cause if it do, I ain't putting it back in the microwave, especially since you ain't say thank you for me doing it the first time." She started pouring Tabasco sauce over the barbecued rib dinner she had bought, sucking her fingers.

"Binkey, something is seriously wrong with yo ass. I can't believe you heated at a nigga because I murked dude's ass before you could, and you seriously gone hold this shit against me, ain't you?" I was really curious to know because I knew she was a beast at holding grudges.

"You damn right. You don't have any idea what I had to go through before you came through that window. Them niggas was pawing all over me, treating me like I was garbage. That made me feel real sick and Tim was the main one, so I was gone make his ass suffer. I wanted to see his face when I cut his dick off and stuffed it in his mouth, but you robbed me of that pleasure." She said pointing a rib at me to emphasize her point.

I bit my boneless chicken breast, "Alright, I guess I ain't look at it like that, my bad. How about next time I let you do all the torture shit and I'll just be the one to punch they lights out when you done had your fun? What you think about that?"

She started talking with her mouth full. "See, you say that now but then when we get to taking care of business you wind up changing everything up. I don't know why you fronting, you know you be thirsty to change something over just like I be, so miss me with that you gone let me do the torture garbage, You know damn well you don't like just sitting back waiting."

I had to laugh at that, she knew me like a book. "I'm saying though boo, you know I don't like you being mad at me."

She smiled. "Aww, here we go with this sappy shit. Boy ain't nobody finna fall for that."

I couldn't stop looking at her. Binky had her hair pulled back into a pony tail, and she'd changed into some boy shorts and a matching pink belly shirt. She looked so beautiful with her hands all greasy, smacking away like she ain't have no manners. I was cheesing like a muthafucka, it was something about Binkey.

"I see you having the time of your life, just smacking away. I'm saying girl, ain't nobody ever taught you no manners."

She started smacking louder, popping her head from left to right, with her eyes closed. Then, she smiled and rolled her eyes. "You know I was just doing that to fuck with you. I remember when we were in the ninth grade, you beat up that Mexican dude cause he kept smacking in my ear. I never forgot that. You used to do some real crazy things over me. What, you think you my knight or something?" She wiped her hands on a few napkins, then handed me a bundle of them.

"You already know you my heart. Don't be thinking just cause you fucking with broads that you ain't gone wind up being my queen. You know how patient us killers are. I'll wait for you until the end of time." Even though that shit sounded cheesy, I meant every word of it. I loved the hell out of Binkey, me and her had been through some real live shit in life, and we always had each other's back, and we always held each other down. Regardless of her sexual preference, I knew that she was my one.

"Boy, you know I love you too, and if I ever cross over, you know I'm coming straight into your arms, I mean that." Her face was serious. "I don't know where I would be in life if I didn't have you." She got up and sat on my lap, then she leaned down and started sucking on my lips, her tongue licking up every trace of barbecue that might have been on there. I attacked her back, loving the way she started moaning and biting on my neck when she straddled, me my hands were all over her plump ass, squeezing and caressing. She stood up and took her belly shirt off baring those perfect brown titties, both nipples were erect, so I attacked them, sucking and pulling with my lips. She began humping her crotch into my dick while she sat straddled over my lap moaning. I picked her up and flipped her onto her back. Her legs were wide open, I saw her camel toe right before she began rubbing her crotch in circles, biting on her bottom lip, watching me strip.

After I was naked as a jay bird, she begged me to stand in front of her, so I did. She grabbed my dick and squeezed it, and I watched her trail her hand in her panties.

"Damn, Roman, you got me crazy with all this damn pipe. I swore to God that I was never putting another dick in my body, but you making it so hard to keep that promise." She started sucking me like a trained professional, all the while her fingers flew in and out of herself, her moaning getting the best of me.

I knew that I wanted her body I had fiened for it ever since we were old enough to know what sex was. I watched her hand like a blur pleasing herself, and something in me snapped. I pulled my dick out of her mouth, pulled her boy shorts to the side, threw her legs on my shoulders and lined myself up to enter her.

She held my shoulder stopping me. "Roman, wait a

minute baby please."

My penis throbbed. I was so horny I thought I would lose it if I wasn't able to slide into her. "Come Binkey, baby." I whined

"Roman if you do this, if we do this, its gone change everything. I mean, I'ma be crazy over you and I'm gone want you all to myself, so you better think about that."

I paused for a second feeling myself throbbing. "That it?"

"That it." She opened her thighs wider.

I slid into her wetness and it gripped me like a glove. That night we were animals. We made love on the couch, on the floor, in the bedroom, against the window while it poured down raining, and we ended the next morning while she was trying to cook, I was hitting that juice box from the back listening to her sexy moans. Binkey had the best pussy I'd ever had in my life, at the time.

Roman

Chapter 12
Roman

Whenever I get tired of dealing with the reality of who I really am, that killer, that cold blooded deviant, I flip the switch and turn to my most respected title, of father. I pulled up to my daughter's school in my brand-new Mercedes Roadster, black on black, with the twenty-six-inch chrome Denaros. I had the hard top dropped so you could see the all white soft leather interior. When my baby girl came out the building, she was talking to her lil friend, but when she saw my car, she took off full speed and ran into my arms. I picked her up and planted kisses all over her beautiful face. Her long curly hair flowed down her back, her brown face was shiny, probably from some beauty product her mother had put on her that morning.

"Daddy, I didn't even know you was coming to pick me up. What's the special occasion?"

I kissed her again then set her down. I reached into the passenger seat and handed her the five foot all white teddy bear I'd bought her. The bear was holding a heart that said, 'Precious Princess'. When Mya saw it tears started coming down her eyes. She hugged me again, saying how much she loved me and how special I always made her feel. As I was helping her get in the Mercedes her friend ran up to the car.

"Mya, you remembered my momma said I could spend a night at your house until Sunday."

"Aww shoot, I forgot about that." She turned to me. "Dad is it okay if my friend Candance comes along with us?"

I looked over to the obviously Asian and Black nine-year-old girl. "Where is your mother at?"

She pointed to a brown Chevy Celebrity three cars

in front of us. I ain't have no problem with her coming along, I just wanted to see who her moms was. "Do you want me to tell her to come over here so you can know she gave me permission?"

I nodded. "Just gotta be sure, lil momma." I watched as she ran over to the car and pointed back to us. Then, I saw the driver's door open and out stepped a woman so fine I immediately began to adjust my jewelry. I made sure the iced Rolex was visible, along with the bracelet on my right wrist. I adjusted my clear lensed Ray Bands and waited for her to approach. She was Black and Asian just like her daughter. They spoke from the passenger's side.

"Hey Mya."

"Hey Ms. Kelly. This is my father right here, his name is Roman. He's taking me out because I'm his baby girl and we would love for Candance to come along with us, if that's okay with you. I mean, she is my best friend and all, and my dad is sure to spoil her too."

Kelly threw her hand on her hip. "Oh, is that right?" She eyed me closely while smiling.

I was tripping on how Mya put the script down. My lil queen had to much of my genes in her. I stepped out the whip and came around to the passenger, side introducing myself. Both girls were watching us as if we were the best movie to come to this the cinema in ages.

"Can I speak to you over here?" I asked her.

"Yeah, cause I see we got two nosey kids on our hands."

I saw Mya roll her eyes, then she began showing Candance her bear.

"First off, I must say that you are extremely beautiful. How is it that our children are best friends, yet I have never been introduced to you before?"

She smiled. "Thank you, you look good too, let me

just be honest. But to answer you question, I am familiar with Rihanna, I never even knew you were in the picture."

I knew she was fishing. "Nall, there is no picture. I make sure she and her mother are well taken care of and that's it. Me and Rihanna are not committed, we are just good friends. Some nights are better than others, if you get my drift." I smiled and winked.

"I do." She blushed, further highlighting her beauty.

"So, what about you?"

"Are you involved with Candance's father?"

"Were off and on. For the most part we try and make it work, but I think he loves the streets more than he will ever love me or his daughter." She sounded defeated.

I continued to listen as she broke down their relationship, it was basically the same kind that me and Rihanna had. I don't think it's too many niggas left that's really trying to do the age old one woman, straight family thing, at least I ain't ran into none in a long time. But I paid attention looking for an opening. When she told me that he was currently locked up and wouldn't be home for another two months I went in.

"Kelly, I wanna take you out to dinner and show you a good time, maybe we can catch a movie a something. You look like you ain't had fun in years."

She smiled weakly. "Is it that obvious? What do you think Rihanna would say about us doing that? I know she going through a rough time and all, especially after losing her sister a lil while ago?"

"Be honest with me Kelly."

"Alright."

"You really don't care how she'd feel, do you?"

She blushed, and that was all I needed to see.

I took the girls straight to the airport where we boarded a flight two hours later, a couple hours after that we landed in Orlando, Florida where we dropped our few things off at the Vizzo Hotel, after that we took a helicopter ride all the way from Orlando to Miami. The girls were mesmerized at the pretty city lights. They kept pointing and oohing and awwing.

The next morning, we spent the whole day at Walt Disney, they must have gotten on every ride in the park and saw every theme. I spent about three thousand there alone on them. After that, we caught a flight to New York where I spent ten thousand a piece on each one of them. I let them pick out whatever they wanted. I got some hot shit for myself, too and made sure I hooked up Binkey real nice. Rihanna sat on the phone telling me exactly what she wanted, so I laced her and got some shit for Heaven and my nephew, I even copped a few items for Kelly. When it was all said and done, I had blown close to eighty gees, but it was all good. I ain't care as long as everybody was happy and got what they wanted. Life was too short to be crunching numbers anyway. I grind just for those moments.

When we got back to Chicago the girls were worn out. I pulled up to Kelly's crib and carried Candance into the house. Their crib was small and cozy. I laid her on the couch and brought in like thirty designer bags. Kelly's eyes lit up.

"You bet not be spoiling her like that. What if she gets used to that treatment?" She said looking astonished.

"Aww, she good. And these are for you." I handed her the three bags from Dolce and Gabbana. "Huh, and this small one too"

She was shocked. She opened the small bag first and pulled out the diamonded tennis bracelet from Levian, the diamonds were chocolate and sparkling. She threw her arms around me and kissed my cheek. "Thank you."

Paid in Blood

She then pulled out the Dolce and Gabbana fits I had bought her, and I knew I had her.

"Alright, I'mma see you later then." I made my way out the door and she jumped into my path.

"Wait a minute, when am I gone see you again?"

"That's up to you. When you wanna see me?"

"How about you go drop your daughter off and come right back, I can tell Candance gone sleep through the night and I have been lonely lately." She leaned forward and licked my ear lobe.

My dick got hard immediately. "Bet, give me a few hours."

I dropped Mya off and kissed my princess on the forehead after she was in her p.j.'s. "Baby I love you, and I will see you tomorrow okay?"

"Okay daddy and thank you." She fell right out to sleep.

I had to fight with Rihanna to get back out of her house. She was trying to put the pussy on me after she saw all them bags Mya had, then I gave her ten of her own. She felt the only compensation she could make was to give me the pussy, so I side stepped her and pulled back up in front of Kelly's crib. Women should already know that nothing can stand in the way of a man and some new pussy.

Kelly attacked me as soon as she opened the door. She had on a all black negligee that was sheer. She jumped on me and wrapped her legs around my waist. I fucked her up against the wall in the hallway with the door wide open. Then I hit it hard from the back on the Welcome mat. She was a beast, talking nasty and calling herself a hot bitch. I was smacking her ass hard while I rammed that pussy and she begged for me to do it harder. By the time we made it to the bedroom, I had gotten off twice. I laid back on the bed while she gave me the best head I done had in a long time, outside of my baby mother.

Chapter 13
Tarig

"I'm 'posed to be spooked to fight this nigga cause he used to be a professional boxer. Yeah aiight, bring it on." I took my shirt off and went to the back of the big laundry storage waiting for the stud to come back there. Peety was beside me, ready for whatever.

The Muslims had gotten word about what was going on, again, and they called for the drama to cease, which meant that things had to end that afternoon. The brothers said they didn't want no drama popping off during Ramadan, which was set to start in one week. The Harper boys were still playing pussy. They refused to fight me or Peety head up, so they hired Champ to step-in and do their dirty work. Word had it that he was a Golden Gloves champion two years in a row before he got locked up. He'd gotten caught with a little heroin and his time was almost up. Supposedly, they had given him five thousand to fight me. I laughed at that. I could never respect a man that couldn't take care of his own business. To me, it was the men in the world like them that were meant to be prey. Now, I ain't personally never took no boxing classes or anything professional. Everything I knew how to do with my hands came from being in the streets and being in the pen. I ain't never bowed down to no man, not even my father, and he used to whoop my ass every night. Whatever was set to take place with Champ, I was prepared for it. I would never fold or crumble.

Peety leaned over toward my ear. "Look Tarig, you ain't gotta fight this nigga. This is my beef, I can handle my own."

I nodded, popping my neck. "I feel that bro, but these niggas put money up on my head, that's disrespectful to me. This stud thinks it's gone be easy, but I got a trick for his ass."

Just then, Champ came into the storage room followed by two well known knuckle heads, Travis and Dean. They were called knuckle heads because they were straight knock out artists. These dudes were vicious, and both were Five Percenters. In the Illinois prison's system, The Five Percenters fell under the Islamic umbrella which meant we all went to worship service together, and though we weren't worshipping the same way, we had a mutual respect for each other. Travis was about five feet seven, real muscular, with a bald head. Dean was probably the same height with the same build except he had real long dreds. They both walked up to me and gave me a half hug. "Peace, God."

"Peace be upon you brothas as well." I looked over their shoulder and saw Champ taking his shirt off. He was about six foot three and weighed close to two hundred and thirty pounds. He flipped his dreds in a pony tail with a rubber band and began shadow boxing in place. I felt my heart starting to beat faster.

"Peep, Tarig, the homie part of our fold, so we just here for moral support and to make sure he don't get jumped. This is business and it's between y'all three." He pointed from me to Peety and backwards to Champ. "After y'all leave out this laundry storage, all this bullshit gotta be squashed."

I nodded and gave him a pound, right as the Muslims filed into the storage twenty deep. "Peace, brothas."

"Peace, Gods."

The brotha, Wazir, stepped forward looking me directly in the eye.

"Ankh, once y'all knuckle up and finish, this has to be over. You understand that?"

I nodded. I was already getting irritated cause it felt

like everybody was trying to give me orders. I ain't like that shit at all. It was one of the reasons why I tried so hard to not get the Muslims involved. I knew that I could take an ass whooping if that was what the occasion called for, but I wasn't the type of nigga that would take that shit laying down. If dude whooped me, I was gone be fighting his ass every single day until I won. I'd never be able to function knowing another man whooped my ass and that's where it ended. I couldn't see that, no matter what the Muslims was screaming.

Champ walked past me and stood in Peety's face mugging him like the boxers do each other while the referee read the rules. I could see a faint trace of worry on Peety's face. His eye started to twitch, and he kept swallowing his spit. I saw him ball his hands into tight fists, staring Champ right back in his eyes.

"First I'mma whoop yo ass, then I'mma whoop his. Nigga, you ready?" He snarled in his face and Travis actually stepped forward and gave this nigga a mouthpiece.

As soon as he did, Peety swung hitting him in the jaw and knocked him down to one knee. I was shocked, then I noticed that he wasn't finishing his attack, so I yelled. "Whoop that nigga Peety, what you waiting on?" Peety was holding his right hand. He had obviously broken his wrist from one punch. By the time he swung with his left, Champ had recovered. He ducked Peety's left hook, came up and gave him two to the ribs with his right hand, and a left cross that spun Peety around before he fell down on the ground bleeding from the mouth where the last punch had landed. Champ stood back allowing him to get up. Peety slowly made his way back to a boxer's stance. Champ charged him again, this time giving him three hard ones to the stomach, a right cross to the jaw and a left upper cut that knocked Peety out cold. He spit blood out of his mouth on to Peety's chest. "Five thousand down and five thousand more to go." He mugged me. "Let me know when you ready."

I knelt down checking on Peety. "Say, blood, wake up! Wake up homie!" I was lightly smacking his face until his eyes opened. Once they did, I knew he was cool, so I started nodding my head. I had my work cut out for me, but I was ready to go at this dude. I silently prayed to Allah to give me strength and to help me overcome this battle against an enemy.

I kept my stance and held my guard. The Muslim brothers nodded and so did the Five Percenters, so we got it on. Champ came right out swinging for the knock out. I ducked his first punch, just to get hit by his second and that muthafucka hurt. He caught me right on the right side of my neck, had he connected with my chin, I would have been out of there, but he missed. I stumbled back a few feet and gathered myself. He rushed me again swinging for the kill, and this time I jumped up and kneed him square in the nose holding the back of his head, then I grabbed him around the neck, stuck my foot behind his legs and flipped him on his ass. He landed awkwardly. I stood back and allowed him to get back up, and the only reason I did that was because it was the rule, had the brothas not been here I would have stomped his lights out. No mercy style. When he made it to his feet, I could tell that he was slightly thrown off his square. So, this time I rushed him, and why did I do that. He side stepped me and caught me twice in my left eye closing it on impact. He grabbed the back of my head and threw me into the side of a big washing machine. All I remember is seeing a blue light before I hit the ground. It took me a minute, but finally I was back standing tall. I was ready to get rid of this nigga, and I knew I couldn't beat him physically, so I was going to have to out think him. I couldn't see out of my left eye at all and my head was throbbing, yet I held my guards up. He got cocky and started laughing.

"I'm gone finish you off now, that's ten gees to the god." He put his mouth piece back in.

I rushed him at full speed, but this time, before he could side step me, I dropped down in front of him and with all my might I punch him right in the nuts. When his head tilted from the blow, I yanked my head upward, head butting him right in the face. He screamed out that I had broken his nose. I didn't care, I wrapped my arm around his neck, putting him in a headlock and I fell to my back slamming his forehead into the concrete splitting it wide open.

The brothas ran over and broke us up. I had blood all over my body. He was out cold. The Five Percenters drug him off and said that it was squashed now. They'd get word to the Harper Boys that there was to be no more feuding. We shook and they departed.

Hood Rich

Chapter 14
Roman

I had just counted two hundred sixty thousand dollars using my money machine. It was all the money that I had to my name besides the eleven kilos of heroin I had hit for two months ago. I was saving them for a rainy day. Chicago always went through some type of drought deep into the summer, so I was gone hold them kilos until that happened and get a nice profit. At two hundred sixty thousand I was alright, but still very uncomfortable. I was feeding a lot of people off of my plate, mostly women, and I kept their asses spoiled, so the crumbs that I had wouldn't last for long. I had to bust a move and I knew just who to call.

My Pops picked up after the third ring. "As Salamu Alakum, son."

"Wa Laikum Salamu, Pop." I returned his blessing. "Pop, we need to sit down and talk business. I'm hungry and need to get something to eat for myself and the family, is your company hiring right now?" I knew my old man was smart enough to read in between the lines.

"Always son. Where are you?"

I told him where I was, and he told me to be at the airport by six pm, there would be a ticket there that would bring me right to the city he was in and he'd be waiting on me when I got there. I hung up.

The plane landed in Houston, Texas. As soon as I got off and made it through the airport, I saw my old man standing outside in a three-piece Armani Suit, with Crocodile shoes. He embraced me with a hug before we climbed into his stretched Cadillac Limo. Inside, the Isley Brothers sang *"Drifting on a memory, ain't no place I'd rather be."* Yeah, I liked that cut, I tapped my fingers on my knee and sung along for a minute. Pops handed me a glass of Crystal and lit one of his Cubans. He started choking immediately, and I still couldn't help laughing. "Pop you smoke that good-good all day and you still wind up choking to death every time you take a pull. You getting old man."

He smiled. "Let's talk business son. What range are you shooting for?" He took a sip of his champagne and handed me the cigar.

I took a pull and inhaled. The dank was so strong I couldn't help but choking. I took five more pulls, almost choked to death and passed it back to my Pops. The high hit me asap. I was feeling righteous. "Pop, I want some real bread, let me hit something that make sense."

He nodded. "Son I got a move for you that's very lucrative, but also very dangerous. If you make the wrong move you could get yourself killed, but if you do everything the right way you could wind up with well over three hundred thousand. I'm willing to pay you fifty gees for the job, whatever you recover is yours, but I know it won't be no less than three hundred."

I ran those numbers over in my head and smiled. "Pop just tell me what I gotta do and fall back."

Chapter 15
Pops

We had been sitting in the dark jazz lounge for two hours, my head was starting to hurt, and my mouth was getting drier by the second. I secretly hated putting my son under the gun, especially when I was dealing with men that were so dangerous. Sitting across from me was one of the deadliest Mexicans in the south. His name was Jorge and he was the boss of the Vegas. They distributed heroin and cocaine all over the south and Midwest. I had made five million dollars with Jorge over the span of eighteen months, but I never trusted him as far as I could throw him. One of the reasons I was having my son close his curtains was because I had a spy on the inside who informed me that Jorge was not taking me into the new year. Meaning that it was his play to have me murdered before the year was out. In this business that we are apart of, it is always most wise to react first and take all threats seriously. I gave Jorge no reason to think that I knew, I had not changed any of my routine, while I was his guest. I came without security and allowed him to think I was strictly at his mercy.

We tapped champagne glasses and saluted to another month of profits.

"You know Armani, I have made you quite a rich man, in such a small amount of time." He sliced the end off of his cigar before lighting it. "One could even say that you owe me."

I took a strong swallow from the bottle of Crown Royal. I always hated to be at another mans mercy. "Jorge, I have to say that doing business with you has been a sight. As far as me owing you, I need to understand what you mean by that."

I looked around the small jazz club. There were a

few janitors cleaning up and getting it ready for its opening that night. Behind Jorge stood his body guard, a skinny Mexican who looked more drunk than dangerous.

"I've been thinking that me moving a few troops over to Chicago would be a great idea, maybe flood some Chi`va over that way, you know expand my hand a little bit."

Just like a greedy ass Mexican. I couldn't disguise the disgust on my face. Had he been anybody else I would have murdered him myself. "That would be a good idea Jorge, if, Chicago wasn't already my turf. Now why would the Vegas wanna step on to a friend's turf?"

He laughed this off. "I wouldn't want you looking at it as if I was stepping on your turf, but more like sharing the apartment with you, something like a room mate."

"A roommate?" I looked up toward his security. I wanted to pop a bullet in his head right then. My temper was fuming.

"Now calm down Armani." He looked up toward his guard. "That name still tickles me." They exchanged jokes before he turned back to me. "Of course, if you consider me a friend you wouldn't mind sharing your turf, after all what are friends for? In fact, he reached on the side of him and slapped two suit cases on the table, opening first one and then the other. "I have four hundred thousand dollars right here as a token of my friendship and partnership. What do you say?"

To me, four hundred thousand dollars was peanuts. In Chicago with the plugs I had, I was easily making that a week, after kick backs and re-investments my take home was about thirty thousand a day. I wanted to tell him to go fuck himself, but I acted as if he had offered me the world. I bucked my eyes out and made it seem as if I couldn't believe my eyes. "Damn, Jorge, you really are serious."

"-As a heart attack."

"You telling me this four hundred grand is mine, with no strings attached." I looked him over closely.

"Absolutely, well, there is one condition."

I nodded. "I knew it was too good to be true."

"No, all I ask is that you surrender the West Side to me. That still gives you three sides and the Suburbs to move freely."

I racked my brain trying to figure out why he wanted the West Side so badly. I knew it was a gold mind, but so were the East, North and South sides. In fact, right then the West Side was in an all out war, it was hard to make money over there during all the chaos.

"What's so good about the West?" I asked scratching my head.

He pulled off of his cigar and blew the smoke to the ceiling. "I have my reasons."

"And how long are you giving me to pull my influence out of the West Side?"

"I'll give you two months, no rush, I'm not thinking of moving out there until then in the mean time, you are free to do what you like. My prices will stay the same, our business will not change."

"Just the Westside, huh?"

He gave me a sadistic sneer, and I knew right then that he saw me as a dead man. I already knew that Jorge secretly hated black folk, but the look he gave me told me everything that I needed to know. I closed both suitcases. "You got a deal."

He reached his hand across the table and I shook it.

As we were crossing the big parking lot back to his limo a red dot appeared on his body guard's forehead right before a hole appeared and he dropped to the pavement. Out of nowhere a person dressed in all black, with a black helmet appeared and put a red dot on Jorge's forehead and then my own. He began screaming through the helmet in broken Spanish. I threw my hands up in the air along with the suitcases. The man continued to scream something in Spanish.

"Jorge, what is he saying, I can't understand that shit!"

"He said to give him the suit cases! Give them to him now!"

"Fuck that!" The man stood back and shot me twice in the chest. The bullets knock me backward against the limo. I fell down and laid perfectly still. He snatched the suitcases from my hands. I heard him continue to scream at Jorge in Spanish, then I heard   *Blocka! Blocka!* A brief pause then, Blocka! *Blocka! Blocka!* "Puto!"

More gun shots were fired before a motor bike was started and then it peeled away. The driver of the limo stood over me, " Senor` are you okay? Senor`, speak to me!"

I faded out, as I heard the driver explaining that a Mexican man had killed me and Jorge. He said the man was screaming in Spanish about paycheck and facing sins. That Santa Maria-.

Chapter 16
Roman

I was loading up my safe when I heard knocking on the front door. I pushed the last twenty thousand in and slammed it, sliding it back into the wall, I secured my safe spot, and moved the dresser back in front of it. The hit had gone more smoothly than I could have ever imagined. I murdered Jorge, giving him six shoots straight to the face. I had to hit my Pops up twice, but I made sure I hit him directly in the vest. I knew he'd be good cause he was wearing that newly designed Kevlar that even prevented armor piercing bullets. The vest he had on was designed for the President, and what is crazy is that Jorge had given it to him. I knew Jorge had to be wearing one too which is why I gave him all face shots at point blank range. Fatality!

I looked through the peep hole and saw Binkey with two Burger King bags in her hands. She must have known I was peeping out because she held the food up. I opened the door and she came in talking a mile and minute.

"I hope you hungry I bought you a Whooper with cheese, extra mayo just like you like it, a large fry, and a Sprite pop." She put the food in the microwave, heating it up.

I came up behind her and tried to kiss her on the cheek, but she moved her head away. I knew right then that there was some bullshit in the air. She only dodged my kisses when she was mad about something. I started trying to remember everything I had done over the last week. I thought about some obvious shit, but I knew it couldn't have been that because she wouldn't have had knowledge of it.

"Damn, I ain't eligible to get no kisses no more?"

Hood Rich

She pushed start on the microwave, turned around leaning on the counter looking directly at me. "Um huh, Roman, you been gone for damn near a week, you ain't called or texted me, I'm sure you done got more than enough kisses and all other kinds of shit from whatever bitch you were fucking." She rolled her eyes, then washed her hands in the sink using the Dawn dish washing liquid.

I came up behind her again trapping her and bit her on the neck, grinding my crotch into her ass that was encased in tight black Michael Kors. She tried to wiggle out of my grasp, but I didn't give her no lead way. I bit her again in the same spot and this time she moaned.

I whispered, "Baby, I was away on business for my old man. He had some business for me to take care of down south. The only reason I ain't call or get at you is because I ain't want no traces of me being down there, you'd be amazed at how the Feds put cases together to convict a nigga, so I played shit real safe. As far as you trying to deny me my kisses, you should know that that shit ain't gone fly." I started sucking on her neck and planting kisses all down her spine.

She moaned and arched her back. "Baby but you had me so worried about you. I hate when you just up and disappear, you know how much I be needing you."

By this time, I was pulling one of her legs out of her Michael Kors. I made her spread them wide and dove in from the back at full speed. Her pussy was wet and gripping me, as if it was trying to hold on for dear life. She slammed back into me groaning deep within her throat. "Oh my god, fuck the shit out of me. Aaaargh!"

We tore the kitchen up. I ate that pussy on top of the table with her ass sitting on a dinner plate. Binkey wrapped her legs around me while I tore that ass up on the counter right next to the microwave, she rode me backwards on the floor while I smacked them caramel globes.

Afterwards, we sat in the tub together with her head laying back on my chest. We had candles lit all over the bathroom. Trey Songz was playing in the background. I relished having her under me. It felt good to have my best friend naked and in the tub with me.

"Baby, can you please tell me how we got here? When did we cross over from being best friends to lovers?"

I ran my fingers through her hair, feeling more relaxed then I had in a long time. I really just wanted to chill. I wanted to enjoy the serenity without explaining how I was feeling, but I doubted she was gone let me do that. Sometimes I felt it was cool to just let things be cause once you started labeling shit, that's when things became complicated.

"Boo, I don't think we 're neglecting being best friends. I think that we both finally realized that this was how it's supposed to be. I been loving you since day one, you know that ain't no secret."

Binkey raised her pretty feet out of the water and wiggled her toes. The water trailed off of her calf and dripped to her thigh. Just watching such a display of femininity, was getting me aroused. She felt it and pushed back on me until my dick was vertical with her back.

"Baby, you ready to go again?"

I wrapped my arms around her and kissed her on the cheek. "Finish what you were saying, baby."

"Aww yeah. No, I know that we are still best friends, but lately I been feeling things for you that I never felt before. It's like all I can do now is think about you and worry about if you're okay. I wish that we could be together all the time, and when we aren't, I start to wonder if you're out fucking with some other chick. And that's fucked up because that never bothered me before, but now it kinda does. Do you think there is something wrong with me?" She turned and looked backward at me.

Ain't no secret that Binkey was my heart, and I already knew that once we crossed that line that things were going to be different, but I had always yearned for this girl. There was just something about her that made me feel so damn good. I had her as deep in my system as she had me and I was never trying to let her go. I'd always kept it real wit her and I didn't see any reason why I would stop.

"Nall, Ma', ain't nothing wrong with you. You just feeling the same way I've been feeling ever since we been kids. I just think the feeling is new to you because you ain't never felt this way for a man before."

She laid her head back into my chest as Trey Songz song about "A super, duper, Jupiter-love" played softly. Binkey was quiet for a moment. We both listened to his lyrics. I tightened my grip around her, and she interlocked her fingers within mine.

"Roman, what if I told you that I wanted you only for myself? What would you say if I said I ain't want you messing with no other females, that mentally I couldn't take imagining some other broad kissing on you or riding your dick? What would you say if I told you that imagining you with somebody else drives me crazy? She squeezed her fingers within mine.

I didn't know how to answer those questions, because all it took was for me to say the wrong thing and we would have been shattered. I wasn't about to lie to her or sugar coat nothing. I had to keep shit real, but I also had to keep in mind that she was fragile and that I was the first male she had ever decided to go there with.

I loved the hell out of her and the last thing I would ever want would be to hurt her.

"Binkey, you know I love you to death, and I ain't never about to lie to you under no circumstances."

"Yeah, I know that. You're the only man in this world that has given me that respect. Go on, baby."

"But you know I still be fucking with other chicks. Not on no love type shit, I just like the thrill of the chase, and then hitting new pussy. I'm not saying that I don't fully enjoy the box between your legs, but its just something in my nature that makes me wanna keep fucking around with different broads even though they don't mean a damn thing to me. I don't want to lie to you and say I'm gone stop doing what I been doing, because what if I don't?"

She stood and stepped out of the tub, wrapping a big towel around her small waist before she walked into the bedroom and finished drying her self off. I followed suit, once I was dry, I slipped on my boxers and watched as she slid her Michael Kors back on without her panties. She buttoned her blouse, neglecting to put back on her bra. I sensed something was wrong, so I walked over and stood in front of her.

"Baby what's the matter?"

She shook her head. "Me, I'm so fucking stupid! I should have known that I wasn't gone be enough for you, but my stupid ass fell for you anyway, that's my own fault. t ain't got nothing to do with you I guess that's just how all men are." She left out of the room making her way towards the front door.

I ran out and blocked her path. "Wait a minute, so you saying I should have lied to yo ass?"

"Roman, please get out of my face." She said without energy.

"Nall, boo, I ain't on no physical shit, I'm just trying

to get an understanding with you. I just kept shit real gangsta with you back there. Instead of you continuing to holler at me like an adult, you straight flipped the script and got on some kiddie shit. Now what would you have preferred for me to do?"

She shook her head, then glared into my eyes. "You're the one person that knew everything that I've been through in life. You knew about all of my past pains and all the shit that my father put me through. You know that I would have never crossed over to a man unless I was in deep love, like I am with yo ass! We done been through so much together, a modern-day Bonnie and Clyde, yet you can't love me enough to be with just me. I feel pointless, I feel lost, and a little bit unloved. I need some time alone so I can think. I'm not mad at you, I'm upset with the situation. But, thank you for being honest, boo." She stepped on her tippy toes and kissed me on the cheek, then stepped around me.

I heard the door close and thought about chasing her, but I decided to give her some time to think because that's what I needed to do as well.

Chapter 17
Seven

I was coming out of the dorms when I saw a drop top, money green, Jaguar pull up to the curb sitting on some all gold Faccius. My sister Brittany was in the passenger seat, waving at me. When the driver got out, I couldn't believe it was my brother. He had on some blue denim Gucci pants with an all black t-shirt, the shoes on his feet were also Gucci and around his neck was three chains iced to death. He walked over to me and wrapped his arms around me.

"What's good, college boy?"

"Damn, big bro, when did you get here?"

"Aww, I been in town for about an hour. But I been watching all your games, Mr. Big Ten player of the year. Dawg, I'm proud of you and best believe moms is too."

I nodded and hugged him again. "Yo. You shining bro! Chicago gotta be treating you good." I said noting his whip and all the jewelry he had on.

"Bro don't let the ice fool you, what you doing here is truly what's good. I'm surviving but everyday I gotta watch my back and sooner or later my time gone run out. This is just a mirage lil brother, the calm before the storm. His face was serious.

I looked over his shoulder. "What Brittany doing in the whip?"

He looked back at her. She singing at the top of her lungs to a Rita Ora hit, popping her neck and all. He laughed. "Aww, I swung by and got her this morning. She done already hit my pockets, we been shopping all day."

I shook my head when we got to the car I leaned down and kissed Brittany on the cheek. "What up', sis?"

"Nothing, just chilling with big bro. N'all, un unh,

why you taking Rita out?"

"Cuz, I gotta hear some T.I., you know ain't nobody hotter than my dude. After we hear a few of his tracks then you can kill us with Rita again."

I jumped in the back seat just as I saw Kendra's truck pull in. "Wait a minute Roman, let me see what my girl wants."

"Yo girl, he turned and watched as Kendra got out of her truck. "Damn!" I heard him say.

"She ain't all that." Brittany hated, "And she ain't giving up the pussy so that broad losing."

"Shut up. Brittany, damn!" Kendra slid into my out stretched arms and planted a delicate kiss on my lips. "Hey baby, how was your day today?"

"Good babe, where are you going? And most importantly, who is this? She nodded her head toward Roman's whip.

"Aww, this my big brother, Roman. He stopped in to scoop me up so that we can spend some time together." She whispered. "But bay-bee, you're entering the big tournament in three days and I ain't gone be able to see you. I thought that we were going to spend these last few days together because we're going to be apart for so long." She said the last part through clenched teeth.

I kissed her thick lips. "Boo I know, but I ain't seen my brother since my moms passed. He lives a real fast life, so every time that I see him it feels like a blessing. I'm going to spend some time wit him, and then later on tonight we can spend some time together."

"Oh, okay, but I am jealous. I miss you so damn much. I need one of your massages, and I want to feel your lips all over me." She whined sounding like a four-year-old.

I smiled. "I got you boo, cause I been needing some

affection too."

That evening with Roman I had the time of my life. We went bowling, then to a pizza joint where we just talked. It felt good being back around my family, I missed my big brother and thought about him a lot. I gave him tickets to the big tournament, and he promised to bring Heaven and the rest of the family. We hugged and I even dropped a tear. I loved the hell out of my brother. I knew the life he lived, but I ain't care. To me he was my hero.

Hood Rich

Chapter 18
Heaven

Damn, I couldn't remember where I'd parked at, so I chirped my alarm until I located my car. I pushed the grocery cart over and let the back of my Expedition when I heard some loud music. I stared to load the truck when the Escalade that was making all the noise came and parked right in back of me blocking me in.

"Uh, excuse me", I said knocking on the driver side tinted window. I waited for the driver to roll the window down and when he finally did, I could not believe how fine this man was. Not only was he driving something off the show room floor that wasn't even released yet, but he and the nerve to be playing India Arie. Damn.

"I'm sorry pretty lady," He jumped out the truck and extended his hand. "I guess I have a confession to make, I'm not too concerned about this parking space. When I saw a woman as beautiful as you, I had to box you in so you couldn't get away. I would love to get to know you."

I smiled, and you damn right, I began getting to know him.

When I got home my son was in the living room with his lil girlfriend. Now first of all, he knew better than to have company when I wasn't home, and secondly, he damn sure knew having a girl in my house was completely out of bounds. I was gone snap on his ass right on the spot, but I decided to play it cool. I didn't care about embarrassing him, but I did care about his feelings.

They were sitting on the floor playing his PS-4. Tarig. was explaining to her what was set to take place on the video game. You could tell that he was intent on her learning fast because his directions were crisp. The whole time he was explaining she looked over at him with a dreamy expression. She obviously didn't care what took place on the video game, all she cared about was being alone with him, that's all that mattered, but of course he was too young to know that.

I shook my head and smiled. That boy was starting to look more and more like his father everyday. He was also aware that he was handsome. My son took great pride in his appearance and stayed in the mirror more that I did, always brushing his hair trying to get the deepest pattern of waves possible. Every time I stood and squinted at my son, he almost always turned into his father. Damn I missed his ass.

"Do you two want anything to drink?"

"Sure ma', can you get us two Hawaiian punches, please?"

I looked toward his lil girlfriend to make sure that would be okay. She nodded and turned her eyes back on my son. "Thank you." She whispered, from the side of her mouth.

Yeah, I was gone have to watch her lil ass. "Elizabeth are you staying for dinner?"

"Aww shoot, I'm sorry momma, I was supposed to ask you if that would be alright." Tarig gave me the puppy dog look. Damn, he looked just like his father.

"That's fine baby, but next time make sure you ask first."

He smiled and gave me that knowing nod.

After damn near six months, I finally was going out for a date. I was a little nervous cause it had been a minute, but I was anxious just the same. I opened up my closet and went through everything twice before I settled on a red Prada halter dress that would accentuate my every curve. Now I wasn't looking to give up no nooky, but I did wanna look good because this man was fine. Umm!

He knocked on the door at seven o'clock, dressed in a crisp Roberto Cavalli suit, all black with red trim, his shoes were Roberto Cavalli as well, wing tipped, all black. When I opened the door, he gave me a hug and I could smell his Bulgari cologne, it was one of my favorite fragrances. His body was chiseled. I could feel every muscle pressing against his suit.

"Wow, Heaven is exactly where I feel like I am when I look at you."

I blushed. It had been so long since I'd received a compliment from a man. "Thank you."

"Shall we?"

"We shall."

We arrived at Alivi Bertolli just as India Arie's fifth track was going off. I really liked that he dug my girl. To me that said a lot about his character. For a man to not only like but understand what that sista was singing about just screamed possibility to me. So far, he was on the right track. For what, I wasn't entirely sure.

The valet opened our doors and he escorted me into the hottest new French restaurant in Chicago. We walked past the patrons waiting for a table and were seated immediately. He pulled out my chair and the whole nine, this was almost too good to be true. After we ordered from the expensive menus, I couldn't help gazing into his dark brown eyes.

He smiled. "Are you okay, you seem a bit nervous?"

"No, I'm fine."

"You sure are." He said with that deep voice.

I blushed again. Damn, I had to get a hold of myself. I couldn't keep letting him know that his flattery was getting to me. I took a sip from my champagne and tried to gain control of myself. I inhaled and nonchalantly blew it out.

"So, tell me why you're single?" I wanted to keep

the heat on him because he had me sweating without the questions.

He picked up his glass and took a nice swallow. "Well, to be honest with you I am just getting back home from doing a tour of duty."

"Oh, you were in the service."

"Something like that."

I noticed him avoiding my eyes. "What do you mean?"

"Well, I'm just getting out of prison."

Fuck, I knew it was too good to be true. As soon as he said that I started thinking about Tarig. He hadn't called me in nearly a week and that was so unlike him. I wondered if he was okay. Maybe I should write him a letter tonight. I started imagining all kinds of crazy things that could have taken place with Tarig. I had zoned out so deeply that it took my date reaching across the table and touching my hand before I came back to the present.

I shook myself out of the trance. "Yes. I'm sorry, what were you saying?"

"Look, it doesn't matter, you wanna get out of here. I'll drop you off if you don't feel comfortable being with me now."

I frowned. "Sweetheart, I'm from the Cabrini Green Projects, I'm used to seeing my brothas go in and out of prison. I'm not going to write you off just because you made a few mistakes, what kind of woman would that make me?" I flipped my hair over my shoulder. "So, what were you in for?" I had to make sure it wasn't for a sex crime or nothing like that, after all I was a single mother with a child.

"I got caught up in the dope game. Heroin was my drug of choice, that's the drug every man in my family has served since its invention. Like my mother always says, it's the Clarks' biggest vice. If my loved ones weren't using it, they were getting rich from it. It's all we know."

"You say, was, has, were and knew, those are all past tense words, so are you saying that all of that is in the past? And remember that either way, I'm a big girl and I'll be able to take the truth. I don't judge, that ain't my purpose in life"

"Nall, ma', I'm still grinding but on a more intelligent level. I gotta feed my family and make things happen for my nieces and nephews. All of their fathers are locked up or dead, so I am all that they have right now, and love don't pay the bills. Grinding do."

I nodded. "I can understand that, it's the life we live, a man's gotta do what he must to survive. I can't knock you for that."

"I appreciate that. So, what the reason you're single?"

"I am single by default. My son's father is incarcerated and won't be home for a little while. I love him, but I have been very lonely as of late, so I just wanted some company, you know, a change of pace."

"No doubt. What I want to know is what kind of pace are you looking for, because when I look at you, I want to slam my foot on the gas and blow through every red light and stop sign." He licked his lips and eyed my cleavage.

I don't know how it happened, maybe time and waiting had finally gotten the best of me, but I found myself back at his apartment where he put me in the tub, then licked my body from scalp to toe nail. I mean he didn't neglect one part of me. His tongue made me cum so much that I fainted. When I woke up, he was pulling me up on my knees then pounding me from the back while he smacked my ass and pulled my hair. I said every curse word known to man as he stuffed me to capacity and rocked me all night.

He woke me up with breakfast, naked, it was the first time I got to see Charles's body and I could not believe God had gave him so many blessings. He had muscles on top of muscles and his dick looked like an elephant's trunk. I hate to say it, but I was hooked and not knowing I was sleeping with a deadly enemy.

Chapter 19
Scooby

"Lay it down! Everybody get on the floor! Any sudden moves and I promise you I'm going to put some hot slugs in yo ass, that goes for anybody!"

I meant that shit too. It was Friday afternoon, and after staking out the small Credit Union for three weeks me and Rallo was finally knocking it off. Chicken was on the floor as one of the customers, and Rallo had just jumped the counter with the black garbage bag. He snatched a white lady up by her hair and demanded she show him where the clean un-marked money was.

"Let's go, two minutes and counting!" Everybody was laid on their stomachs, noses pointed to the floor. So far so good. As Rallo began dumping money into the bag, Chicken got up and ran out of the bank, making it seem like she was escaping. I faked as if I was going to chase her then stopped. I knew she was going to pull the car around. "If anybody else tries that shit, I swear to God that I'mma kill em'!"

I heard the horn beeping outside. "Let's go! We out right now!"

Rallo jumped over the counter with his Barack Obama mask on and fled out the door, I followed closely behind keeping my eyes on everybody. "Thank you, ladies and gentlemen, you may now go on with your evening."

"Ahhhhhh!" Rallo screamed. "Ahhhhhh, we did that shit, nigga!" He kept hugging me and picking Chicken up kissing all over her face.

"Boy put me down, just because the mission was a success did not mean that your toothpaste was. Please stop kissing on me."

I snickered at that. Chicken was always busting

119

Rallo's chops and today was no different. I had the money in neat piles across the table and so far, I was at three hundred thousand a piece. In the end this was the best lick we had hit in a long time and Rallo couldn't contain himself. He was already on his cell phone trying to order a whole kilo of dope. He said he was gonna smoke until his heart burst, and I believed him. I simply shook my head.

"Nigga, you a damn fool." I grumbled.

He stopped dancing and frowned. "Blood, what's the matter?"

"Yo stupid ass just robbed a credit union not fifteen blocks from here and now you on the phone getting ready to blow twenty-five thousand dollars right out the blue. Yousa` stupid son of a bitch and when you get caught, muthafucka, you bet not say my name." I spoke my peace without looking up at him, I was recounting my money.

"Yeah, Rallo, Scooby does have a point, how is that going to look?"

"Aww, come on, Chicken, not you too. Damn y'all don't ever let me have no fun. I just wanna get high."

I stood up. "Blood, that's your money, you can do whatever you wanna do with it, but after it's gone, just make sure you stay the fuck away from me because them pigs gone be at yo ass, you can believe that kat daddy." I dismissed him. An hour later, after talking some sense at his ass, him and Chicken left.

There was a pounding on my back door. "Who is it?"

"It's Amanda, Scooby, I need to use your phone its an emergency!"

I let her in, and she ran right to the phone. After five minutes of being on it, she broke down crying. She finished her conversation, hung the phone back up and began bawling her eyes out. I stood transfixed, I didn't know what was going on or what I was supposed to do in that instant. Suddenly, Amanda ran from the couch and wrapped her arms around me and buried her head into my chest. I held her while she cried and cried.

After a while Amanda was able to tell me that her grandfather had passed away after fighting cancer for two years. He was her closest grandparent and she didn't know what she was going to do without him. She started to cry again I wrapped my arm around her shoulders and held her tight. I told her that everything was going to be alright and that whatever she needed I would make sure she got it.

"Scooby." She whimpered.

"Yeah, baby."

"Do you think that after I go upstairs and put the kids to sleep that you could come up there and hold me through the night?"

I know my animalistic instincts were supposed to kick in, and I was supposed to look at this as an opportunity to get in those panties, but I actually felt sorry for her. I knew that she was alone and didn't have nobody to protect her. I kinda felt that it had to suck so I decided right then I would be there for her.

"Of course."

I waited an hour, then locked my back door and slipped up her stairs. You see, we stayed in a duplex. In order to get into her apartment, you had to come through the back of the house. My lower residence entrance was in the front, and her upper residence was in the back. So, when I left out my back door, it led to some stairs that stopped at her locked entrance. I took the keys out of my pocket she had given me and entered stepping right into her kitchen.

Amanda was standing there with one finger held in front of her lips. "Shhhh, they just fell asleep. Come on."

She grabbed me by the hand and led me through the dark house which looked identical to mine with the exception of the black leather scheme she had going. Her place was well furnished and looked cozy.

In her bedroom she dropped her silk robe and revealed herself in a short stain black negligee. "Come on." She climbed into the bed and held the covers back. I slid out of my Timberlands and started to crawl in when she stopped me. "Take these dirty pants off, I just washed theses sheets."

I stripped down to my boxers and white beater, sliding in behind her small frame, and feeling her snuggle back into me. "Ummm, you feel so good. Now hold me tight."

And I did.

The next morning, I awoke to her snickering. I opened my eyes and slowly she came into view. Amanda was all dressed and looking as beautiful as ever. She covered her mouth with her hand and pointed. I looked to where she was pointing and saw that my penis was sticking straight up through my boxer hole. I mean standing tall too. I tucked him back up and rose, putting my pants on.

"Scooby, I appreciate you being here last night that really meant a lot to me."

I started putting my Timms on ignoring her and still a little bit embarrassed.

"Did you hear what I said?" She leaned into my face.

I nodded. "You're welcome, lil lady."

Amanda sat directly on my lap and looked me in the eyes. "For some reason I think I got a crush on you because every time I'm around you I always feel some type of way." She wiggled a little in my lap causing my dick to wake up again. "Damn, that feels good." She got up and closed her bedroom door, then knelt down between my legs and pulled my Johnson out. Before I knew what was going on, she was giving me the best head I'd had in years.

When I came, she swallowed everything, then stood wiping her mouth. There was light knock on her bedroom door. "Momma. Momma."

"Shit, Scooby, can we get together later on? I gotta drop them off at my sister's house for the weekend, then try and figure out how I'm going to get the money for this rent and some clothes for them."

Amanda looked as if she had slumped into a deep state of depression. She opened the door and picked her son up onto her hip. He waved at me and I smiled. "What up lil homie?"

"Are you my daddy?"

I took a deep breath and blew out the air. "No, I'm mommy's friend, we're going to go buy you some toys later, then we're going to go pay some bills and stuff.

All he heard was toys because he kept repeating the word over and over again until his brother came in two years younger saying the same words over and over. Amanda eyed me closely as if she was angry. She put him down and he and his brother ran into the dining room.

"Why you tell him that, you know he's going to be expecting those now? And what do you mean pay some bills?"

I grabbed her arm and sat her on the bed. "Calm down, lil lady. I meant everything that I said. We gone go pay whatever bills you've got. Then we gone go get them some clothes, food and toys. I got you. You ain't gotta do this shit alone. I'll hold you down until your man come home, don't worry."

Tears began falling from her eyes. Amanda wrapped her arms around my neck and laid her head on my chest.

"Thank you so much. I was seriously lost I ain't know how I was going to make ends meet."

That night I received a call from Rallo that would change my entire life and cause me to lose Amanda's and her children's lives in the sickest of fashions.

Chapter 20
Roman

Eerrrrhhh! "Fuck nigga, get the fuck out of the car right now or I'mma blow yo head off!"

Damn, I was caught slipping. The masked nigga jumped out the van and slammed a double barrel shot gun to my temple demanding I get out of my brand-new drop top Jaguar. This car wasn't even a month old yet. It took every ounce of will power in me not to go under my seat and grab my burner. If I did that, I was sure he would have splattered my common sense all over the dash board. The crazy part about the whole situation is that I wasn't scared. I was more pissed off than anything. How had I not seen that big ass van approaching? I was too caught up in T.I.'s c.d. 'Paper Work'.

I threw my hands in the air. "Aight homie, I'm reaching for the door handle, I ain't on shit, you got me." I started to open the door when he grabbed me by the head and flung me out onto the pavement. Then somebody jumped out of the van wearing a black ski mask.

Before he jumped in the car with his partner, he yanked the chains from around my neck. "Give me this shit!" He snarled then upped what looked like a .380 and shot me twice in the chest area. The last thing I remembered seeing was him jumping into the passenger seat of my Jag and smoke coming from the tires as they pulled off.

It felt like my chest was on fire, somehow, I managed to get up, then I was running. I almost got hit by two cars, yet I kept running, until I finally collapsed. When I woke up a real pretty lady was looking down on me. I felt something cold smearing across my chest and I thought I was dying. So, If I was dying then the pretty lady must've been my angel. My vision was hazy, and it was hard for me to focus. I looked up at her and she kept smiling. The more I concentrated the easier it was for me to focus, until I understood that I was laying on my back on a couch. I was laying in somebody's living room.

"There you go Sugar, you gone be okay. You just had a lil minor mishap, but everything is going to be okay." My angel cooed.

My mouth was dry, making it hard for me to talk. When I finally did, my words came out raspy. "Am I dead?"

She laughed out loud, her pretty face taunting me. "No baby, but you would have been had you not been wearing this." She held up my military issued Kevlar vest. I saw that it was a little damaged, but still in good shape.

As if on instinct, I slid my hands over my chest and stomach feeling for holes and discovering none. My heart started to beat faster and faster. Suddenly I sat up. "I'mma kill them niggas!" I was pissed off and my anger was getting the best of me. I didn't even know who the robbers were, I just knew that they had left me for dead, even after I'd given them my whip, to me that was enough to make any man go insane.

"Young man calm down. First you should thank God that you are alive before you go on and enact your revenge. Praise His holy name for giving you this blessing. She rubbed my forehead and stood up.

My first thoughts were, damn she was strapped. This older sista had a body that those movies from the seventies and eighties repped. She even looked like that caramel, Pam Grier. I watched her walked into the kitchen and fantasized what sexing her body would be like. She had on some tight white bell-bottomed pants and a white blouse. Those pants hugged her like a second skin.

"Say Ms...?"

"Baby, just call me Chicken."

"Say, Chicken, you right, I gotta check myself. I really appreciate you taking care of me and inviting me into your home."

"That's okay. You collapsed right there on my porch, so I just pulled you on in here. When I saw that you had gun shot wounds but no blood I kinda figured you were wearing a vest. That's why I wound up icing your chest and abdomen down. I ain't call no authorities, figuring that you'd be against that. I didn't know what the circumstances were for you being shot so I played it safe." She went into the kitchen and came back out with a tall glass of lemonade and handed it to me.

"Thank you, Chicken, is there anything that I can do for you? Can I give you some money or something for keeping it so gangsta wit me?"

She smiled and waved me off. "N'all, Sugar, I'm good. Just promise me that you won't go back out there and kill nobody. After all, you have to remember that God spared your life, so you owe somebody's mother to spare their child."

I shook my head. "Nall, Ms., I definitely feel what you're saying but I can't promise you that. I live in a dog eat dog world. For me to say that I'll never change nobody again would be a lie to you, and I feel like I owe you more realness than that. So, ask me anything else."

She paused, taking in what I'd just said. "Then, how about you go to Church with me this Sunday?"

"Don't do Churches, I am a Muslim."

She nodded. "Well, I'm cooking Sunday dinner after church, how about you come by and have Sunday dinner with me for the next three Sundays, just so I can make sure you're alright."

"No pork?"

She reached and stroked my cheek. "No pork, I promise."

I called Binkey, and when she showed up, I jumped in her Navigator and told her everything that had happened. She kept cursing and hitting her steering wheel as she drove. She began swearing bloody murder, before it was all said and done, tears were coming down her cheeks. No matter what I said, she just would not stop crying. When we made it into her apartment she ran right in straight to the bathroom where I heard her purging her guts. I knelt beside her holding her hair back and rubbing her back. When she finished, she gargled with Scope, and trotted slowly to the living room and slumped on the couch. I sat beside her trying to console her.

"Baby, don't trip, it's good. I'mma catch them niggas who put heat to me, you already knew that. Ain't no need in you getting yourself sick over this shit, you know it's part of the game."

She shook her head. "That ain't why I'm sick."

"Then what's the matter?"

"Roman, I'm pregnant. We are going to have a baby together. I have known for about two weeks. Well it's been confirmed for two weeks by my doctor. So, Congratulations." She sat on the couch crying with her hands clasped over her face.

I was in shock. Pregnant! How the fuck did that happen. I didn't ever see myself having any more kids. The life I lived was already crazy enough. I was having a hard time processing this information. Then I thought about how much I cared about her, and all the stuff that we had been through and the thought of having a kid with her started to make sense. If I had ever considered having another kid, I knew I wanted it to be with her.

"Okay, Ma', so let's take care of our responsibilities and raise this child together."

She took her hands from her face and glared at me. "Together?" Roman you just got done telling me a few weeks ago that I wasn't enough for you. Now, why all the sudden would you change your tune, just because I'm pregnant? What makes you think that I will be enough for you now?"

I stood up. "Hold on Binkey, don't start that bullshit again."

"Oh, now its bullshit?" She said dryly.

"Yeah it's bullshit. You came out the blue with these provisions of me being with just you. When we started doing our thang together you already knew what type of nigga I was. So, what, since we fucking now, this tiger gotta change its strips?"

She got into my face. "Nigga, I know you ain't standing here talking to me like I'm Rihanna or one of them other punk bitches! You betta fall back and realize who it is that you talking to. Treat me with the respect that I'm due or we gone tear this muthafucka up, and I mean that shit!"

She glared at me with her jaw clenched. I could not believe that her lil ass was actually ready to knuckle up with me, and she knew I was a fool with my hands. I walked up on her and pressed my forehead against hers.

"Shorty, so what you saying? What you don't think I'll get all in that ass for how you coming at me?"

She pushed me in the chest hard. "Nigga, I wish you would! What's good then? What you waiting on?"

To say my blood was boiling would be an understatement. Never in my life had I ever hit a female but in that moment Binkey was pressing her luck. She took her ear rings off and threw up her guards acting as if she was really ready to throw down. I took a deep breath, and visualized my seed being nourished in her womb. I thought back on all that we had been through and my anger subsided.

"Binkey, I love you too much to ever put my hands on you. You're right I was wrong for how I came at you. You deserve better than that."

She was bouncing on her toes with her guards up. My words caught her completely off guard. "Say what?" She was confused.

I reached out and grabbed her arm. "Boo, come here and sit down. Look, I'm glad that you pregnant. I got you. Whatever it's gone take for me to do to make sure you and our child are always straight, I'mma make sure I make it happen. But you gone have to give me some time to adjust to everything. Rome wasn't built over night."

"Damn, I know boo, but I didn't have a chance to adjust to anything. I woke up nauseous, next thing I knew I was confirmed pregnant. We have to put our priorities in line right now. And we gone have to stay out of them streets. It's impossible to raise a child and run the streets. We gotta choose either or."

Without a shadow of a doubt I knew she was talking directly to me. She had dropped a lot of stuff on my brain and I needed some time to clear my head.

I spent that night laid up with her. We had some of the best sex that we'd ever had. Afterward I lay holding her trying to imagine her being my one and only for the rest of my life. Could I do it? Was I man enough? I didn't know the answer to those questions.

The next morning, I copped a BMW 530i, black on black with all white leather interior. It took me five hours in all to get my system and t.v.'s hooked up into it, and for my rims to get added. By the time I got done with all of those pit stops it was four in the afternoon. I went and got my hair cut and my goatee lined up. On my way out the barbershop I saw Kelly coming out of the beauty shop across the street. Just as I was sliding into the driver's seat, she called my name.

I waited until she crossed the street, then she hung on my car door peeping around at the insides. "Damn, boy, how many cars do you have?"

I smiled. "How you doing, Kelly?" She was looking real good after getting her hair done. She had on one of the Prada outfits I had bought her, a pink number that made her look youthful.

"I'm doing fine, just wondering why it's so hard for me to get in touch with you. What, you forgot my number or something?"

"Nall, Ma', but you know how the streets are. I can't be caught playing all the time, some time gotta be reserved for work."

"I hear that."

Just then a cab pulled up behind her, she turned around and threw up one finger. "Well that's me right there. So, when am I gone see you again?" She leaned forward so that her breasts damn near fell out her tube top. They looked real ripe and delicious. Her perfume went straight up my nose, further drawing me in.

"Shid, where you on your way to now?"

She smiled devilishly. "What you want me to bless your new whip?"

"Shortie, do I even have to ask?"

The next thing I knew, I was punching the whip to one hundred twenty120 while Kelly gave me super brains. I weaved in and out of traffic on the highway with one hand while my other one forced her to take all of my dick, and she was a champion. Then she slipped a condom on it and I had to lean to the right while she rode me screaming in my ear about how deep the dick was in her. She licked all over my neck and sucked on my ear lobes until she came riding me full speed and splashing deep in her guts.

We got back to her crib and had three more rounds before I was exhausted. She came in the room and fed me a frozen pizza she had cooked in the oven and I felt like a ghetto king.

Chapter 21
Roman

I'd almost forgotten about hitting up that nigga, Moeshe until I bumped into him at the club three months later. I had been laying low trying to get more in tune with myself when Binkey out the blue decided that she wanted to go out. She said that she had been cooped up indoors ever since she found out that she was pregnant and that she was starting to get bored. After arguing with her about her giving me so many mixed signals we wound up hitting Club 713. It was one of Chicago's hippest night clubs. You absolutely had to know somebody that knew somebody for them to let you just walk to the front of the line and by-pass security the way that we did. They didn't even give us a second glance, just simply moved out the way. I had two twin .9 Rugers on me and Binkey had her Machete and a .380 on her. We weren't looking for any trouble, but at the same time we were prepared for anything. I kept one pistol in the small of my back and the other one in my ankle holster. Binkey kept her machete and .380 in her purse which she kept on her at all times.

We checked our coats in but that was all. They knew who my Pops was so they ain't sweat me or Binkey with how Chunky we looked about the waist and purse. The club was cracking. It was dimly lit, strippers on three stages making them dollars. It was packed but order was maintained. Everybody had a place to sit, or dance if that's what they were feeling. We slid beyond the velvet ropes into V.I.P into a booth right in front of the center stage where two strippers were catering to the girl on girl fantasy. Both were fine ass hell, thick, with no inhibitions. They were basically fucking on stage. I saw one stripper slide her two fingers in the other one more than once and I couldn't take my eyes off of the scene.

Binkey leaned over and whispered. "Baby close your mouth before something fly in it and you choke."

She was joking. My mouth wasn't open all like that, though I can't lie, I was feeling what they were doing. I felt Binkey slide her hand into my lap unleashing my Johnson. Then she was giving me full on head while I watched the strippers 69 and suck on each others' pussy lips. She had my eyes rolling in the back of my head making them loud slurping sounds. I made eye contact with one of the strippers and she gave me a knowing look and ran her tongue across her lips. When she crawled over on to her knees and I saw how fat her pussy was. I splashed and felt Binkey swallow all of me, then end by kissing on my helmet.

"Better now, baby?" She laid her head on my shoulder and continued to watch the show.

That's when I scanned the club and saw a group of niggas coming into the V.I.P section. I stood alert and Binkey perked up. She followed my eyes and saw the group of men coming our way. They were ten deep with so much jewelry on it was like they robbed a jewelry store. Moeshe led the way looking like Rick Ross, behind him his goons followed until they were seated two booths to the left of us. As soon as they sat down a minimum of nine strippers flocked to their table and they pulled out stacks of money preparing to trick something good. The waitress sat five bottles of Ace of Spades on their table and I saw Moeshe pat her on the ass to which she smiled. He handed her a twenty for a tip, then she walked away nearly breaking her hips from her switching.

"Baby, ain't that Moeshe right there?"

I nodded. "Yeah that's that nigga." I didn't see JJ with him, he was probably working the hood while his boss lived the good life for a minute. Ever since we had knocked off Tim and Moe, Moeshe, and his right-hand man, J.J had moved into that territory and were eating good. They had young dope boys all up and down the blocks with every prescription on the ready. Instead of them solely pushing pills, they pushed everything and anything an addict would want. The fact that they were getting paper didn't mean nothing to me, I wasn't no hater. The only time I clocked another nigga's cash was when I was preparing to take it. I really didn't have no beef with these kats other than the fact I was pretty sure they had something to do with my baby momma's lil sister getting changed. The streets said that Moeshe gave the order for that entire turf to get rained on for a week straight. I felt deep in my heart that it was during one of his fire storms that the shorty D had been hit up. I still needed something concrete to confirm my suspicions. These were major players in the game, so for anybody to go at them you had to come correct or else yo ass would get whacked.

I glared at the niggas on the sly, just watching them do their thang. Then, another kat was crossing the ropes into the V.I.P and I saw Moeshe get up and hug him while introducing him to everybody. I'd never seen him before, but he had a crazy aura radiating from him. As he was hugging the last goon our eyes caught and for some reason, he began looking oddly familiar. I just couldn't place his face though and that was unlike me, usually when I saw a face that was familiar, I instantly connected it to a place and time, but for some reason I was falling short at that moment.

He sat down and a thick assed stripper sat on his lap while he palmed her juicy titties. They sparked a few Dutches, and popped bottles, obviously relishing in the good life. I had a million and one thoughts running through my head. I was strapped right then but it would have been crazy to run over there and start letting bullets fly, plus I had to confirm what I already suspected. I was also caught with another dilemma because after hollering at my old man, I found out that Moeshe and J.J was keeping shit one hunnit and hitting my old man with twenty bands every week, and that was simply because they were respecting the game and paying homage to my Pop. And that wasn't it, they were also copping all of their heroin and ecstasy from him, so whacking them two would seriously hit my Pop's pockets. Knowing him it probably wouldn't hurt him that bad, but it also confirmed the fact that I had to have proof before I went at these studs.

"Roman, I hate when you get quiet, that means you got a whole bunch of sick stuff running through your mind." She interlocked her fingers within mine. "Baby tell me what you thinking so I can know what's good. Is we on business right now or what?"

I snapped out of my zone after weighing the pros and cons. "N'all, boo, we good. I'mma hold fast and do a little more digging. I just can't go at them studs on a bogus whim. The streets gotta be barking by now, so I'm gone see what's the word. Until then let's enjoy the rest of our night." I grabbed a thick, dark skinned stripper by the hand who was on her way past us. "Say, li'l momma, how about you give my lady right her a nice lap dance.

Chapter 22
Roman

Another three months had passed, and I'd hit numerous capers out of town for my old man, Indiana, Iowa, Milwaukee and even Detroit. I didn't know what my Pops was on but within the last ninety days I'd made a little over four hundred thousand which was more than a breather for me, so I was coasting.

My sister called me that morning and said she wanted me to stop by to help celebrate my nephew's thirteenth birthday. So, I found myself at the mall with pregnant Binkey picking out my lil homie some gear and video games. By the time we left the mall she had twenty bags and only five of them were for my daughter and nephew. Two were for me, and the rest were for her spoiled ass. We got back to the crib and got dressed. I threw on a whole Tom Ford fit, black, grey and white, with the matching retro-8 Jordans. My waves were hitting, and I smelled like Fan di Fendi cologne.

Binkey, even though she was six months pregnant, still looked good and was just starting to get a lil belly. She had on a black and grey halter dress from Lord and Taylor, with some flat Stuart Weitzman's on her feet. She still looked fine as hell and her skin was glowing. She'd put diamond rings on every finger, both wrists and an ear lobe. I knew she was trying to show off, so I just shook my head.

I snapped on my gold Rolex with the diamond face, a pinky ring, and a custom-made herring bone that had diamonds all over it. I looked in the mirror and gave myself the stamp of approval.

Binkey pushed me out of the way. "Dang, boy, get yo ass out of the mirror. You too damn connected already."

"Whatever, shorty, I'm just making sure I look good. This how my moms raised me." I slid my hand over my waves one more time feeling those deep ripples. "And I know you got some nerve to be talking that conceited garbage. How you gone push me out the way just so you can come stand yo ass in the mirror"

She laughed. "Boy gone, I'm a girl, I'm supposed to live in front of the mirror. Besides I gotta look the best as I can, I already know your lil girls gone be there." She rolled her eyes.

That was true, it was a fact that Rihanna was going to be there with my daughter and as far as I knew she hadn't caught wind that Binkey was pregnant or that me and her was messing around now. I'd just given Rihanna some gross, X-rated sex two weeks before. I mean we went all out. So, as far as she knew I was still a bachelor, doing me.

"Look, Binkey, don't get over here and get to acting all crazy and shit. You know Mya gone be here and I want her to love you more than she already does. So, keep that at the forefront of your mind for me because her opinion is very important to me."

"Calm down, Bill Cosby. We straight. I'm not gone embarrass you in front of her. But I hope you done gave yo lil exes the same tongue lashing that you giving me. This is a two-way street, long as I get respect, I don't have no problem giving it." She went back to curling her hair.

"You heard what I said."

"Yep, and you heard me, too."

When we pulled up in front of my sister's house the sun was beaming so hard, I almost put the top up on the BMW. The humidity was even worse. It was in the middle of June, yet it felt like August already. Heaven had cars parked in front of her house and in the driveway. So, we wound up parking two houses down after the woman watering her grass said it was okay for us to park there. I looked over at Binkey and she looked like she was dying form heat exhaustion.

"Baby, you straight?"

"Wheew, lets get in here already, it is too hot to be outside."

As we were stepping on to the porch Heaven was coming out the door with a bag in her hand. When she saw me, she screamed out, dropped the bag and wrapped her arms around me, hugging me so tight as if she was trying to squeeze me to death.

"Oh my God, Roman! I can't believe you actually showed up."

"What you talking about, I ain't never missed one of my nephews' birthdays since he, and I don't intend on missing none either." I picked her up in the air, planting kisses all over her before putting her down. She was blushing and smiling at the same time. Then she looked past me and saw Binkey holding my nephews' gifts.

"Aw hell nall, I know that aint Binkey." Heaven wrapped her arms around her, then backed up, looking at her with a confused expression on her face. "Uh Binkey, girl now I don't mean to be rude or disrespectful but it look like you're pregnant, or either you hiding something under your shirt, and it got be the latter because I know you don't mess with men like that, do you?"

Binkey looked at me. She bugged her eyes out. "Uh, Roman, don't you got something to tell your sister?"

I laughed. "That's how we doing it?"

Heaven looked up at me wondering what was going on.

"Sis, you going to have a nephew in about five months."

Her eyes got bucked. "Shut up! You two? Oh my God, I'm so happy!" She wrapped her arms around Binkey again, then rubbed her stomach. " Girl, it's about time y'all got together." Then she punched me in the arm. "And why is this the first time I'm hearing about this, Roman?" There was a sign of hurt in her voice.

I tried to hug her, but she pushed me away. "I'm sorry sis, but you know how I don't like to jinx stuff. I had to make sure that everything was all good first."

"Yeah whatever." She led us into the air-conditioned house, and it felt like I'd been saved when I felt that cool air. "So, does that mean that yall are together finally?"

I gave her that look that told her she was putting me on the spot. And she gave me a look like she knew that and didn't care. Binkey stood in front of me and crossed her arms waiting on my response. I felt concerned and didn't know what to say. Just as I was about to put my foot in my mouth, my nephew saw me.

"Uncle Roman!" He ran and crashed into me and I picked him up hugging him.

"What's good, li'l man?"

"I can't believe that you're here!"

I put him down. "You know I couldn't miss out on you turning thirteen. You practically a man now.

"Hey! Don't tell him that crap, he still my baby." Heaven leaned down and kissed his cheek.

"I got you some presents too. I had to go hard for you. Everything is fresh off the presses. You can thank your Aunt Binkey too." I nodded in her direction.

"I was finna say, dang when was yall gone acknowledge me." She bent down waiting for a hug from Tarig Jr.

He hugged her. "Thank you, Auntie." He analyzed her middle. "Are you pregnant?"

She smiled. "Yes I am. Me and your Uncle Roman

are going to have a little boy."

"I'mma have a boy cousin!" He was excited and overjoyed looking from Binkey back up to me.

"Yeah lil homie, how you love that?"

He threw his arms around both of us, then Binkey handed him his five bags.

The house was crowded with mostly teenagers or preteens. Drake played out of the speakers in the background while my sister did her thang in the kitchen. The table had a huge cake on it with a picture of Lebron James's Cleveland jersey. I knew that was my nephew's favorite team and player. He had developed good taste from me.

I wondered aimlessly through the party helping out Heaven with drinks and setting the table. Heaven was running back and forth to the Barbeque grill, so I decided to step outside and give her a hand. That's when I found out that she wasn't the one working the grill, but there was some stud on it. As she was heading back inside, I stopped her and asked who he was.

"Aww that's my friend Charles, we been talking for some months now, nothing serious, just passing time until Tarig get back home. So, don't start tripping."

"I'm saying, where you meet this stud at? Do Tarig know that dude is around my nephew? And do Tarig Jr. like him?"

Heaven frowned up. "Roman, do not forget that I am a grown woman and do not have to answer to nobody. My life is not supposed to stop just because my man is serving a bid. Best believe I make sure he stays straight and don't need for nothing while he in there. As far as him knowing about Charles, what would be the purpose of that? That would only give him something to worry about when he should be focused on getting up out of there. And to answer your last question, Tarig Jr. does not have a problem with him. He knows who his father is, but he respects my right to be happy until his father comes home."

I had to respect my sister for how gangsta she was keeping it with me. "Alright, Heaven, I'mma respect your position, but I'm letting you know right now that if homie ever get out of line, I'm clapping his ass. Tarig's my brother, and he loves the hell out of you. Everything he did when he was out here was for you, so don't let that stud make you forget that."

Heaven nodded. "I won't." She finished carrying the latest batch of barbequed brats into the house.

I decided to go holler at the cook. I couldn't see his face that clearly because he had sun glasses on, but as I got closer, he started to look oddly familiar. I squinted my eyes and he must have known that I was trying to see who he was because he took his shades off and before me was the same Kat from the Club a lil while ago.

He extended his hand and I shook it. "What's good my name is, Charles."

"'m Roman, Heaven is my sister, and my heart." I made sure I emphasized that last part. This stud looked like he was known for beating woman. Standing there with a black wife beater on all ripped up and shit.

"Yeah, I know who you are, she talks about you all the time."

"Say homie, why do you look so familiar to me?"

"Honestly? Me and you were locked together in Statesville. They called me Champ back then, you the one who knocked out that Italian for breaking the Muslim's formation. Back then I was just coming in for a heroin case. They'd found heroin in my locker at one of my fights."

That's where I knew this nigga from. I knew he looked familiar. I remembered the Italian punk who had walked between our formation while we were congregating on the rec field. That's something that you never do. You never break some groups formation in prison I don't care who you are. The Italian had connected family so he thought he could walk around like he owned the place. As soon as he broke our line, I was on his ass. That was my first fight in prison, but not my last. After that, the Muslims were at war for two months straight. I stabbed up so many white folks I started to get addicted to it. It was back then that I developed my love for murder. After Tarig came through the gates it was really over, we started finding reasons to go at the white folks. We mostly targeted racist Italians and white Supremacists. After a while, they begged the Muslims for a treaty.

"So that's where I know you from. Wasn't you at the club with Moeshe them?"

"Yeah, Moeshe's my nephew. Since I been home, that's who I been eating with, Lil homie, was just a petty hustler when I got locked up back then. But, just like the streets talk, prison talks too. I found out my blood was killing the streets of Chicago, eating real good. I'm proud of him." He continued flipping the meat.

"No doubt, I'm familiar with the homie. You fuck with J.J too?"

"Yeah, I watched him grow up from a lil old cry baby. Now he out here bussing heads. If niggas don't move around for Moeshe, J.J the one that air out the whole block, neighbors and all. Lil homie ain't got no remorse." He flipped the ribs over on the grill and swiped a barbequed brush across them.

"Yo, I been trying to get my footing, Blood. It's hard out here. I'm trying to hit the ground running on some hustle–hustle. What's it gone take for me to be able to get down with the crew?"

He laughed. "It is crazy out here. I'm fresh out and still trying to get my footing. What's your hustle of choice, though?"

"I grind with that boy."

"Me too, tell you what, let me pull some strings and figure some shit out and I'll get back with you. Maybe we can get out here on some shit for ourselves. I'mma be at you though."

Now that that was situated, I eased back and played my position. I knew that he was a key piece to getting to Moeshe, and J.J. As I said before I had a lot more research to do, but he was a pawn that needed to be manipulated. So, I kept him close and over the next few months I gained his trust, and his respect.

Chapter 23
Roman

The first incident happened while we were in the midst of dropping off a shipment for Moeshe. We had been at my sister's house indulging in one of her Friday night fish fry. Heaven was famous for getting down on Fridays ever since she had gotten her own place when she turned seventeen. Ever since then, she made it her business to out do herself every Friday, and I must say, so far, she had. We sat around the table with bottles of Louisiana Hot sauce, Tabasco sauce, and even barbeque sauce. She'd whipped up spaghetti with Italian sausage, freshly made garlic bread from scratch, green bean casserole, and blue Kool-Aid. For dessert was seven-up pound cake with glaze and strawberry ice cream. When I say my sister threw down, that's exactly what I mean.

There was so much smacking going on around the table that the neighbors had to have heard us. Me, my daughter, Binkey, my nephew, my grandmother, Heaven, Rihanna and Charles, but by this time we were all calling him Champ. I felt kinda guilty because I had not been out to see Tarig in nearly a year. Heaven said that he was back in the hole and wasn't able to have visitors except on the tv screen, and I knew how demoralizing those were, so I decided to just wait until he got out before I went and saw him. Every time I saw Champ sitting across the table from Heaven, I thought about my mans and felt like I was betraying him by allowing dude to sit across from his family. I aint dig that shit one bit, but I knew for the moment that it was necessary and there was nothing I could do because Heaven had her mind made up. She was the type that when her mind was made up there was nothing you could tell her. I respected the fact that she was happy and

145

that she kept a smile on her face. I guess that should have meant everything, but I had that loyalty drum beating at me. All I could think about was Tarig.

The only thing that took my mind off of him that evening was when Rihanna pulled me in the bathroom and broke down crying. "You mean to tell me that you bringing your pregnant girlfriend to our Friday fish fry's now?" She asked.

"Listen Rihanna, don't start this bullshit."

"Fuck that, Roman! You bring this pregnant ass girl here to eat over my sister house like that shit's cool. Don't you know that theses dinners are special to me, that us coming to Heaven's dinners use to be one of the special pillars of our relationship, I thought that at the very least we was gone be able to keep this event between you, me and our daughter. Damn, nigga, what, I don't matter no more at all or something?" Tears poured down her pretty face.

I took a deep breath and blew it out harshly. "Damn, Rihanna, what the fuck do you want from me? Don't I take care of you and make sure our daughter stays straight? Don't I pay all ya muthafucka bills and your mom's rent? Every time you call me, I break my neck to get to you no matter where you are, so what the fuck is it that you want from me? What you feel like I got that I ain't giving you or our daughter?"

She shook her head from side to side, silently crying. "You just don't get it do you? Yeah you take care of everything financial so that we never need or want for anything. And yes, you are a damn good provider in every single way. As a man, I gotta say that you are stand up. But boy, I swear it's so much more to being a man than that." She poked me in the chest, until I smacked her finger away.

"Say, shorty, we ain't gone do the physical thang.

You can make your point without putting your hands on me."

"Roman, what happened to us being a family? What happened to when I give you a daughter you gone make me your wife, huh? When did you start looking at me different? When did you start seeing me as a female who deserved to be a statistic? A single mother, unwed, and in the ghetto? When did I become just another broad you banging?

"Rihanna, you don't really want the answer to those questions, do you?" I raised, my eyebrow, looking her over.

"You damn right I do. In fact, I think that's the least that I deserve."

"First off, you still mean the world to me. I -"

"Nigga, fuck the sugar coating part. Just hit me straight on, no chasers, I'm a big girl."

"The last time I got locked up Re Re, you ain't hold me down like you was supposed to. You kept me in suspense. Heaven had to bring my daughter to see me, because your ass was missing in action. You kept an excuse about everything. Over-all, you wasn't on shit. Yea you one hunnit when I'm out and the getting is good. But, when I'm down and I need somebody to hold me up, you never there. That's when I figured out that you weren't that ride or die chick that you always screamed you were. Shorty, pressure busts pipes, and pressure shows you who a person really is."

She sat down on the edge of the tub and put her hands over her face, beginning to cry hard. Then, as suddenly as she started, she stopped mid-whimper. She stood up and walked into my face. "Do you have any idea what I had to go through to provide for your daughter when you got arrested? If you remember correctly, they raided the whole house and took every penny we had in there. They also took my little stash that I was saving for a rainy day. A stash that didn't have nothing to do with whatever it was that you were doing. So, with you gone, and that gone, I was unemployed, because I was young and used to depending on yo ass.

I admit I was simple minded and with a daughter to raise. How do you think I faired out here in these streets, huh? Answer that! Nigga you in theses streets more than traffic jams, so you know how hard it is. But I ain't got no muthafucking gun, or no sack of dope. I ain't have none of that shit all I had was Mya, and a whole lot of bills. So, you expected me to spoil yo ass in prison, take care of our daughter and myself, and all of the bills! With what skills? Because I had none.

You taught me only to receive, you never showed me how to go out and get it on my own, so I was lost and had to learn a lot of things along the way while bumping my head time and time again. But I never fell, and I was always there for yo ass. It may have not been when you wanted me to be there, but I was damn sure on time. So how dare you disrespect me by saying what you just said. Nigga, man up and keep shit real for once. You been feeling her, and you been wanting to be with her, I was just a place holder, a broad to keep you busy until you got the one you really wanted. At least be man enough to tell me that." She looked me deep in the eyes and curled up her lip. "As much as I love you Roman, boy, I hate you just the same. You broke my heart. I mean you seriously got me all fucked up. I think from here on out I might be the one to fuck with women because you men really ain't shit. Just promise me that you gone continue to be a good father to our daughter and that she will never come second to your new kid. Please?"

The words, "I promise.", were all I could say.

So, after me and Champ picked up the shipment

from J.J, we hit the road. We were traveling with five kilos of heroin, and fifty thousand ecstasy pills, the destination was a city up north by the name of Milwaukee, Wisconsin. Most people didn't know where Milwaukee was located, when you said Wisconsin all they thought about was the Green Bay Packers or Lambeau Field. But that was a three-hour drive from Milwaukee. Milwaukee is a city where all the pimps, macks, rappers and niggas with major money gotta visit at least twice in their lives. This small city located in the upper crust of the Midwest, is known for flashy hustlers, flamboyant foreign cars, and fast women who are so beautiful, but deadly at the same time. These women were hip to the game and would set you up quicker than an FBI informant.

Milwaukee was known for being small, and for having cold blooded killers as young as twelve years old. This city loved when you underestimated their gangsta, it made serving your death warrant so much easier. When it came to the streets killers always relished what came quick and easy. Stupidity was at the top of the list.

I was familiar with the city because, growing up, my old man had established himself out there. Plus, my mother ran a restaurant, or should I say she over saw one of her trade marked restaurants up there. But with my Pops, after he moved up there for a few years I'd spent three summers with him and a few winters, it was during these times that I found out the kats in Milwaukee played for keeps. My first summer I personally witnessed two of my lil homies get they heads blown clean off by a kid younger than us, at that time I was fourteen. The next summer, three of my close homies got shot up, and I got popped twice. The third summer I shot three niggas and killed two dudes. I wasn't about being on that receiving end again. I learned my lesson the first two summers. After I was shot the first time, I made sure I came up from Chicago prepared every summer after that. Milwaukee was also the place where I sexed my first older lady.

I turned to Champ as we passed the Green sign telling us Milwaukee's population. "Bro, you ever been up this way before?"

"Nall, but this shit should go sweet. Theses niggas up here ain't on shit, what kind of name is Milwaukee? He laughed.

And I didn't. "Say, Champ, yo, we ain't gone sleep on these niggas. I'm familiar with this city and I'm telling you they some animals up here. Most of them is from the Chi or somewhere down south. Don't think we going to deal with some preppy white boys cause I'm telling you it ain't gone be that type of party."

He turned off the exit on North Avenue and headed North. "Aw, baby, you ain't never gotta worry about me not being on point. I know we dealing with some animals if my nephew fucking with them, we just gone handle business as usual."

When we got to 27th, I saw him make a right and he stayed on the busy street. "Say where we going anyway?"

"26th and Burleigh."

Aww yeah, I knew that kats over there were real grimy. Suddenly, I was wondering how much business Moeshe had done with these dudes. I knew the area well because my mother's restaurant was right on 27th and Burleigh, which was one block over from our transaction destination. They called this area the zoo, cause wasn't nothing but low-life, wild animals parading about the area, and that included men and women. The area was drug infested and completely run down. It reminded me of parts of Chicago that even the killers avoided.

We came up to the BP station on 27th across from my mother's restaurant. I could see the waitresses working on the inside going about their day as usual. My grandmother would be selling this restaurant over the next few weeks. Just seeing it made me think about my Queen. Man, I missed her.

I knew it had to be bullshit in the air when they directed us to turn into the alley in the back of 26th street. When the Benz pulled into the dark alley there were five men that came out of the shadows and approached the whip. I started wondering what type of niggas did business like this.

A short, stocky, dude with a bald head came to the driver's side with a neck full of gold jewelry on. "Say pull that car into that garage right there." He pointed to a vacant garage in the middle of the alley. Champ nodded.

"Bro, make sure the trunk of the car is inside the garage and not the front." I tightened my vest on me and cocked both .40Glocks. I had that feeling.

After we followed their directives, we parked and got out the car: It was pitch black, you could only see in front of you because there was one street lamp a little way down the alley. I counted six dudes, and they all looked strapped and grimy. I ain't feel right. My stomach started doing summersaults.

The stocky leader walked up to me. "What's up player?"

We definitely were in Milwaukee, everywhere you went there was somebody calling you a player, or a mack. I nodded. "Shit, what's good, joe?" I returned my own Chicago lingo at him.

"Foe, I can't call it. I ain't never seen y'all before.

Y'all must be new. How long y'all been down with Moeshe?"

Champ cut in. "Say, homie, Moeshe my nephew, this my mans, everything kosher, lets get this shit on the road."

The stocky leader looked offended. "Hold on, say player, you ain't in Chicago no more. Nigga, I run this. This my turf, I'll say when the show gets on the road, and until I do, ain't shit moving. How I know you niggas ain't the Feds?"

The Feds, aw this stud was definitely tripping. I kept feeling like something wasn't right. I looked around at his goons and all them studs looked like killers and not drug dealers. You could tell the difference between the two, and these dudes was definitely not the latter, so I decided to throw a bait out there.

"Yea you right home boy look, we in yo world, homie. We just want to get this deal over and done with because we got a few more drop offs in the city."

His face scrunched up. "Where at?"

I smiled. "That ain't important."

He laughed. "So, you mean to tell me that yall fucking with other niggas in the city, and yall ain't made them drops yet? Damn, that means that that trunk loaded with merchandise then."

I saw him give the eye to one of his goons and before he could reach to up his weapon, I blasted the stocky nigga twice in the face and shot his goon once through the neck. I had the stocky nigga's brains all over my face, but I kept shooting. I hit another stud who upped a gauge and got one blast off before I caught him twice through the forehead. I chased another nigga catching him four times in the back. A few goons got away. I searched all of them niggas and only found pistols, no money. These studs were never looking to "buy" no product, this shit was a hit from the beginning, but just to be sure I searched all around the garage for a duffel bag or anything that the money could have been in. I came up with nothing. I took my shirt off and wiped my face then burned it. Champ peeled the Benz out of the garage, and we burnt rubber taking alleys all the way down to Center street which was about four blocks. Just as we were ready to hit the Avenue, we saw two more of the goons.

Champ parked and jumped out the car. "I got this." I watched him run up on the heavy-set goon and pop him once in the head, the front of his face exploded, and he fell forward. Then he chased the skinny man before popping him six times. He went back and dumped three more slugs into the first one and we peeled out of there, and out of Milwaukee.

Hood Rich

Chapter 24
Roman

"I searched all of them mafuckas, ain't none of them kats have no money on them, that was a hit from the beginning bro, trust me."

"How did you know though? What made you beat them niggas to the punch?"

"Bro cause this dope dealing shit ain't my forte, whacking mafuckas is. I know when the heat is on, and they were finna change us to get to that dope. I baited that fool. Any hustler ain't gone care who else dope you got long as you got his. When they found out we had more than his dope in the car, his eyes got big as saucers. He gave his lil henchmen a signal that I caught and it's because of that signal that we still alive and them niggas is changed over."

Champ looked over to me and gave me that eye that said thank you and he appreciated me saving his life. "Yo, I owe you fool."

"Never joe, it's all apart of the game. What we need to find out is why would J.J send us on that mission if he didn't know what was really good with them niggas."

"Yo, I'm all over that. I'mma meet with Moeshe personally about this. I got a feeling that there more to it that meets the eye."

Back in Chicago, he dropped me off at Binkey's crib and told me that he would be in touch. Binkey opened the door looking tired. She leaned forward and kissed me on the cheek, then walked off straight into the kitchen.

"Boy, go take a shower, you smell like death and gun powder. I'mma heat your food up and then you can tell me what's good."

I did just that. After I got clean and told her what

happened she simply shook her head. "But that's what I love about you, you have those great killer instincts. My only worry is when God gone take those away from you, and essentially take you away from me. I keep having the worst of dreams every night, whenever you aren't in my bed holding me all night." She crossed herself like the Catholics do, then started mumbling under her breath. I noticed that she was starting to do that a lot lately.

She put on some old Keith Sweat "*I will never do anything to hurt you.....*" I nodded my head at those lyrics and pulled her in close to me, wrapping my arms around her. "Ma, what matters is that I'm alive." I kissed her forehead.

She laid her head on my chest as we stood there. "I know that baby, but for how long?" I felt her holding me tighter.

Keith Sweat sang on, but her question played over and over in my head, uninterrupted.

The next day Mya came over, so Binkey and I took her out to Noah's Ark. Of course, she had to go get her lil friend Candance which meant I had to dodge a million and one questions as to why I hadn't gotten back to her mother. After everyone I answered, she popped a new one, until she killed me with her last statement.

"Roman, I don't know how you gone take this, but I'm pregnant." She shoved some papers in front of me that she had gotten from her doctor. "It must have happened the first few times we were together. I wasn't gone say nothing until I was absolutely sure, but I am, so."

I kept re-reading the paperwork over and over in my head. I had so many thoughts going through my head I thought my brain was going to explode. The first thing I did was call Binkey into the house. I was so damn defeated. I prepared myself for the outburst that was sure to come from her as soon as she found out what I already knew. Kelly stood across the living room looking at me as if I had lost my mind, but the only thing I was thinking about was getting all this shit over and done with right now I couldn't believe that I had allowed myself to be so reckless. It's like they say, sometimes the penis does get the best of a nigga. Binkey came into the house smiling, when she saw my expression everything in her face became distorted. She put her hand over her stomach and looked worried. She looked from Kelly back to me.

"Roman, what's wrong?"

I shook my head, then handed her the paperwork. She scrunched up her face and sucked her teeth. She flipped the paper over to see if any writing was on the back then shoved them into my chest. "And? So, what's the purpose of you handing me this?" Her tone was starting to get harsh.

Kelly tried to fade into the kitchen. I called her name and told her to chill. "Look Roman, I don't want no drama, I was just trying to let you know what the deal was."

Just then Mya and Candance ran into the living room laughing. "Daddy, what's taking you so long? Can we go already, you know if we get there late, we gone have to wait in long lines for everything, then you going to get mad and it'll ruin everybody's day." She was tugging my shirt, the sunlight reflecting off of her beautiful face.

"Baby, go wait in the car. Me and Binkey will be there in just a moment, let us finish discussing grown folks' business." I kissed her on the forehead.

She smiled. "Come on Candance, we gotta do what my father says or else we won't be going nowhere." She grabbed her friend's hand and they slowly walked back outside.

As soon as they left, it was like the whole aura of the room changed. Binkey quietly closed the door behind them. Then she opened the curtains so we could keep an eye on them. Once she was secure that they would be okay, she walked up to me and swung trying to slap me, but I ducked. Then she upped a machete from the small of her back and ran full speed at Kelly, who fell then got up in a hurry to get away.

Before she could catch her, I caught up to Binky and wrapped my arms around her from the back. She turned her neck and bit me on the shoulder. Pushing her head backward, she tried to head butt me.

"Girl calm yo ass down, what the fuck is wrong with you?"

"Let me go Roman, you cheating son-of-a-bitch! You better let me the fuck go, now! You're hurting me and the baby!"

I didn't know if she was telling the truth or not, so I eased up just a lil bit still very conscious of the machete in her hand. "Binkey drop that big ass sword boo. Calm yo ass down so we can talk about this shit like adults!"

"Like adults?" She wiggled with all of her might trying to break loose. When she realized that I wasn't going to let her go she began to calm down. "Alright, I'm cool Roman, just let me go."

I stayed conscious of the machete, but by that time I was so irritated that I was ready for whatever, if she was going to try and get at me with that blade, then I'd just have to go for what I know. I definitely wasn't gone let her slice me with that mafucka. I let her go.

She straightened out her dress, and turned around slowly to face me, still holding the big blade. "Who is that bitch, and when did you start fucking her? Was it before or after me Roman, and look me in the eye while you answer these questions?" I had never seen her angrier than she was at that moment.

My expression was blank. You know that face you get when you know yo caught, and it ain't nothing you can do about it besides keep it real and face up to your wrong doings. I felt like that. I felt like the world was crashing down on me and there was nowhere for me to run. What's crazy is that I also felt humbled, and ready to get everything over and done with. I had never told Binkey that I was ready to settle down with just her or nobody else for that matter. Don't get me wrong, over the last couple weeks I had been definitely considering certifying her as my one, but in my own mind I had not done that as of yet.

"Boo."

"Nigga, don't boo me right now. Just tell me what's good, and remember, you looking me right in the eye."

I gazed into her brown beauties and kept shit one hunnit. "Both. I fucked with her before and after, but not since. I've gotten serious with you in my own heart."

Her expression was one of confusion. "What you mean by that? What do you mean that you ain't messed with her since you got serious with me within your heart?" She spat nastily.

"Come on Binkey, you know my life style, shorty. You know how I get down. I ain't never considered being with just no one female until I met you. And boo, even so, it still has taken some will power within myself to be faithful to just you. This shit is a process."

Her eyes bugged out. "A process. Oh, okay, so it's hard for you to keep shit one hunnit with me? Its that hard for you to be faithful, when you supposed to love me, and been loving me ever since we were kids. Why do you get to pick when to be faithful, but as soon as you see a nigga glance my way you be ready to kill his ass?

So, imagine what you would do if I lay on my back and let some nigga jump up and down between my legs. And what if I told yo ass that I was going through a process." Tears were pouring down her cheeks at this point. "Then, you got the nerve to get this girl pregnant, when I'm standing here already pregnant with your child. I just don't get it."

Damn, I hated when a woman I cared about cried. That shit broke me up, especially when I was the cause. So many excuses were running through my head, but none of them made sense. I wanted to wrap my arms around her, but I felt that would have been a mistake. I was stuck. "Binkey, baby, listen." I knelt down in front of her. "I fucked up boo. Huh." I tilted my head back and exposed my Adams apple. "Go ahead, Ma'. Do you! Boo, I fucked up, I betrayed you, so correct that shit." I swallowed, prepared for her to change me over.

She grabbed my chin with tears in her eyes and raised her arm all the way in the air with the machete in it. "I'm sorry boo." I saw her face become distorted, then she bit into her bottom lip and was coming down with the machete at full speed.

To Be Continued...
Paid in Blood 2
Coming Soon

Submission Guideline

Submit the first three chapters of your completed manuscript to ldpsubmissions@gmail.com, subject line: Your book's title. The manuscript must be in a .doc file and sent as an attachment. Document should be in Times New Roman, double spaced and in size 12 font. Also, provide your synopsis and full contact information. If sending multiple submissions, they must each be in a separate email.

Have a story but no way to send it electronically? You can still submit to LDP/Ca$h Presents. Send in the first three chapters, written or typed, of your completed manuscript to:

LDP: Submissions Dept
Po Box 870494
Mesquite, Tx 75187

DO NOT send original manuscript. Must be a duplicate.

Provide your synopsis and a cover letter containing your full contact information.

Thanks for considering LDP and Ca$h Presents.

Hood Rich

Paid in Blood

Mimi

A HUSTLER'S DECEIT 3

KILL ZONE **II**

BAE BELONGS TO ME III

By **Aryanna**

THE COST OF LOYALTY **III**

By **Kweli**

SHE FELL IN LOVE WITH A REAL ONE **II**

By **Tamara Butler**

RENEGADE BOYS **III**

By **Meesha**

CORRUPTED BY A GANGSTA **IV**

By **Destiny Skai**

A GANGSTER'S CODE **III**

By **J-Blunt**

KING OF NEW YORK V

RISE TO POWER III

COKE KINGS II

By **T.J. Edwards**

GORILLAZ IN THE BAY III

De'Kari

THE STREETS ARE CALLING II

Duquie Wilson

KINGPIN KILLAZ IV

STREET KINGS 2

PAID IN BLOOD 2

Hood Rich

STEADY MOBBIN' **III**

Hood Rich

Marcellus Allen

SINS OF A HUSTLA II

ASAD

TRIGGADALE II

Elijah R. Freeman

MARRIED TO A BOSS III

By Destiny Skai & Chris Green

KINGS OF THE GAME II

Playa Ray

Available Now

RESTRAINING ORDER **I & II**

By **CA$H & Coffee**

LOVE KNOWS NO BOUNDARIES **I II & III**

By **Coffee**

RAISED AS A GOON I, II, III & IV

BRED BY THE SLUMS I, II, III

BLAST FOR ME I & II

ROTTEN TO THE CORE I III

A BRONX TALE I, II, III

DUFFEL BAG CARTEL I II

By **Ghost**

LAY IT DOWN **I & II**

LAST OF A DYING BREED

BLOOD STAINS OF A SHOTTA I & II

By **Jamaica**

LOYAL TO THE GAME

Paid in Blood

LOYAL TO THE GAME II

LOYAL TO THE GAME III

LIFE OF SIN

By **TJ & Jelissa**

BLOODY COMMAS I & II

SKI MASK CARTEL I II & III

KING OF NEW YORK I II,III IV

RISE TO POWER I II

COKE KINGS

By **T.J. Edwards**

IF LOVING HIM IS WRONG…I & II

LOVE ME EVEN WHEN IT HURTS I II

By **Jelissa**

WHEN THE STREETS CLAP BACK I & II III

By **Jibril Williams**

A DISTINGUISHED THUG STOLE MY HEART I II & III

LOVE SHOULDN'T HURT I II III

RENEGADE BOYS I & II

By **Meesha**

A GANGSTER'S CODE I &, II III

By **J-Blunt**

PUSH IT TO THE LIMIT

By **Bre' Hayes**

BLOOD OF A BOSS **I, II, III, IV, V**

By **Askari**

THE STREETS BLEED MURDER **I, II & III**

THE HEART OF A GANGSTA I II& III

By **Jerry Jackson**

165

Hood Rich

CUM FOR ME

CUM FOR ME 2

CUM FOR ME 3

CUM FOR ME 4

An **LDP Erotica Collaboration**

BRIDE OF A HUSTLA **I II & II**

THE FETTI GIRLS **I, II& III**

CORRUPTED BY A GANGSTA I, II & III

By **Destiny Skai**

WHEN A GOOD GIRL GOES BAD

By **Adrienne**

THE COST OF LOYALTY

By Kweli

A GANGSTER'S REVENGE **I II III & IV**

THE BOSS MAN'S DAUGHTERS

THE BOSS MAN'S DAUGHTERS II

THE BOSSMAN'S DAUGHTERS III

THE BOSSMAN'S DAUGHTERS IV

THE BOSS MAN'S DAUGHTERS **V**

A SAVAGE LOVE **I & II**

BAE BELONGS TO ME I II

A HUSTLER'S DECEIT I, II, III

WHAT BAD BITCHES DO I, II, III

By **Aryanna**

A KINGPIN'S AMBITON

A KINGPIN'S AMBITION **II**

I MURDER FOR THE DOUGH

By **Ambitious**

166

Paid in Blood

TRUE SAVAGE

TRUE SAVAGE II

TRUE SAVAGE **III**

TRUE SAVAGE **IV**

TRUE SAVAGE **V**

TRUE SAVAGE **VI**

By **Chris Green**

A DOPEBOY'S PRAYER

By **Eddie "Wolf" Lee**

THE KING CARTEL **I, II & III**

By **Frank Gresham**

THESE NIGGAS AIN'T LOYAL **I, II & III**

By **Nikki Tee**

GANGSTA SHYT **I II &III**

By **CATO**

THE ULTIMATE BETRAYAL

By **Phoenix**

BOSS'N UP **I , II & III**

By **Royal Nicole**

I LOVE YOU TO DEATH

By Destiny J

I RIDE FOR MY HITTA

I STILL RIDE FOR MY HITTA

By **Misty Holt**

LOVE & CHASIN' PAPER

By **Qay Crockett**

TO DIE IN VAIN

SINS OF A HUSTLA

Hood Rich

By **ASAD**

BROOKLYN HUSTLAZ

By **Boogsy Morina**

BROOKLYN ON LOCK I & II

By **Sonovia**

GANGSTA CITY

By **Teddy Duke**

A DRUG KING AND HIS DIAMOND I & II III

A DOPEMAN'S RICHES

HER MAN, MINE'S TOO I, II

CASH MONEY HO'S

By Nicole Goosby

TRAPHOUSE KING **I II & III**

KINGPIN KILLAZ I II III

STREET KINGS

PAID IN BLOOD

By **Hood Rich**

LIPSTICK KILLAH **I, II**

CRIME OF PASSION I & II

By **Mimi**

STEADY MOBBN' **I, II**

By **Marcellus Allen**

WHO SHOT YA **I, II**

Renta

GORILLAZ IN THE BAY **I II**

DE'KARI

TRIGGADALE

Elijah R. Freeman

168

Paid in Blood

GOD BLESS THE TRAPPERS I, II, III

THESE SCANDALOUS STREETS I, II, III

FEAR MY GANGSTA I, II, III

THESE STREETS DON'T LOVE NOBODY I, II

BURY ME A G I, II, III, IV, V

A GANGSTA'S EMPIRE I, II, III

Tranay Adams

THE STREETS ARE CALLING

Duquie Wilson

MARRIED TO A BOSS… I II

By Destiny Skai & Chris Green

KINGS OF THE GAME II

Playa Ray

Hood Rich

BOOKS BY LDP'S CEO, CA$H

TRUST IN NO MAN

TRUST IN NO MAN 2

TRUST IN NO MAN 3

BONDED BY BLOOD

SHORTY GOT A THUG

THUGS CRY

THUGS CRY 2

THUGS CRY 3

TRUST NO BITCH

TRUST NO BITCH 2

TRUST NO BITCH 3

TIL MY CASKET DROPS

RESTRAINING ORDER

RESTRAINING ORDER 2

IN LOVE WITH A CONVICT

Coming Soon

BONDED BY BLOOD 2

BOW DOWN TO MY GANGSTA

Paid in Blood

Lightning Source UK Ltd.
Milton Keynes UK
UKHW021905090222
398445UK00010B/2299